REX

'Convincing and full of observation about the countryside and sheep-farming, the setting against which the dog learns all he has to know about living.'

Daily Telegraph

'You will know what a sheep trial is like, even if you have never visited one, after reading this book. You will learn a lot about sheep-farming and about survival, but you will not know you are learning. Everything is fascinating to Mrs Stranger. She sees with eyes that are clear and fresh, and finds each sight new and stimulating.'

Yorkshire Post

REX

Joyce Stranger

CORGI BOOKS
A DIVISION OF TRANSWORLD PUBLISHERS LTD

REX

A CORGI BOOK 0 552 08141 8

Originally published in Great Britain by
Harvill Press Ltd

PRINTING HISTORY
Harvill Press edition published 1967
Corgi edition published 1969
Corgi edition reprinted 1969
Corgi edition reprinted 1972
Corgi edition reprinted 1973
Corgi edition reissued 1976
Corgi edition reprinted 1979
Corgi edition reprinted 1982

This book is set in Intertype Baskerville

Corgi Books are published by
Transworld Publishers Ltd,
Century House, 61–63 Uxbridge Road,
Ealing, London W5 5SA

Reproduced, printed and bound in Great Britain by
Cox & Wyman Ltd, Reading

To Jocelyn Oliver

CHAPTER ONE

THE bitch had come to the fells for sanctuary. She was a Border collie, her black coat marked by a flake of white on her neck, a patch of white on her left shoulder, and distinguished by one white forepaw. She was footsore, limping over the heather, her tongue hanging loose as she panted. She was looking for a dry warm place in which to lie, and hide.

Her master was a shepherd, on a small hill farm that was now more than fifteen miles behind her. He ran a few sheep on the hills, and kept only one sheepdog, the little bitch, Nan. He hoped to buy a dog, fully trained and able to herd as well as Nan, but he had no inclination to teach it himself, and no intention of paying the high prices asked for a good animal.

So that when Nan had pups, it was a disaster, and he drowned them at birth. He could not spare her from the hills, and she, though she mourned bitterly, was too well trained to disobey her master's bidding, and she followed him wearily, desolate with loss, and lay at night on the straw in her kennel, remembering her pups, nose on paws, and eyes forlorn.

A second litter followed the first, but Nan could not be spared from the hill for three weeks, locked away from all dogs. Now her third litter was due. This time her maternal instincts outweighed her loyalty, and she left the flock just before the birth, intent on getting away, to a place where she could have her young in peace and rear her pups. She knew her master would take them away from her otherwise.

Far behind her, the shepherd was furious. He had searched all day, calling and whistling, and been forced to herd the sheep alone, a lengthy and almost impossible task. He felt bitter as he went to his home, knowing that now he would be forced to part with at least twenty-five pounds for a well-trained dog, able to take on where Nan had left off. He'd have no more bitches. He had no other regrets. The sheepdog, to him, was a mere necessity, a tool of his trade, to be ordered to do his bidding. Affection did not enter into the partnership. Perhaps, if it had, Nan would have been willing to sacrifice her third litter.

Her progress was slow. She needed a lot of rests, and determination to put as much distance as possible between herself and her home kept her moving until the moon was high above her, a thin shred of light in a cloud-mottled sky, showing the world black and forbidding. It was an unfamiliar world, for she was always locked up at night. She moved warily, aware of lurking unseen dangers from other animals, and from the sly foxes that, she knew, came to prey on ailing or new-dead lambs, and might well fancy a new-born pup.

A small wind rustled the heather, a dry ghostly sound of stealthy movement. It stirred the long hair of her coat, and the scents that were borne on it reminded her that she was hungry. Her master fed her late at night, when her work was done, and fed her meagrely, on porridge or bread and milk. Meat was rare, and she craved it to help her feed the pups within her.

She knew she had no time to hunt. She needed shelter, and she cast around on the hill, finding nothing but bare ground under clumped heather. Beyond her, she saw rock, a grim outcrop jutting starkly into the sky. The craggy surface was puddled, and she drank deeply, afterwards lying with her nose on her paws, recovering her breath.

Shelter was vital. The moon hid. Thin rain wetted the rock, and damped her coat and she stood again, sniffing the wind, puzzled, longing for a place out of the wet, a place where she could find a bed on which she could bring her pups to birth.

Nan sighed deeply. Pain was racking her, and soon there would be no more time. Fear of the night and its dangers made her speed over uneven ground, swerving on to soft pine needles under dense trees, momentarily protected from

8

rain that was now lessening. There were strange scents on the breeze. The rankly choking smell of fox, the enticement of rabbit, the trace of a squirrel, curled high in its drey, the terrifying memory of a hunting weasel, teasing on the air.

By the time she had left the shelter of the trees the rain had stopped and the moon once more lent light to the sky. Her vision was blocked by a drystone wall, beyond which there was the comfortingly familiar smell of sheep, though they were strange sheep, not those that she knew at home.

Momentarily the herding urge dominated her immediate needs, and then, as pain needled her again, died away, and she skirted the wall cautiously, rustling through the ditch, frantically seeking a safe place for her pups.

The hollow tree stood alone in the heart of an open field. It had been blasted years before by lightning, and, in its time, sheltered many small beasts. Nan saw it, and went towards it, desperate, now looking only for protection from the wind close against its ample trunk.

She circled the tree, automatically seeking the side away from the wind. The thin moon lighted the hole at its base, protected by knotted roots which held thick pockets of loamy earth in which grass grew rankly, masking most of the entrance.

Nan crouched and sniffed at the hole. The only scents were faint, from creatures that had left there long ago. She crawled inside, finding protection from the wind and rain and a dense mat of dry leaves that would make an ample bed. She rested, and long before the moon had dipped behind the hill, or the last faint stars dimmed out of the misty sky, her four pups were born.

They were sturdy, and she licked them clean. She lay, nursing them, fierce with pride, thwarted motherhood dominant at last. The tiny warm bodies pressed close against her, blind-eyed, whimpering, as they lost the source of rich milk, and found it again, nuzzling eagerly, minute clawed paws moving against her. That day, she could not have enough of them, and not even her growing hunger urged her from them.

When dusk shadowed the hills next day, she left the pups,

9

knowing that she must have food. Twice she went back, nosing them, anxious to make sure that they were safe and then, reluctantly, she ranged the fell, always within sight of the tree.

Luckily, rabbits were there, cropping the scarce grass, bounding in games of tag that ended abruptly with each participant sitting, sniffing the air, alert for danger.

The scent of rabbit was strong. Nan was impatient, but her sheepdog cunning helped her stalk along the wind, coming with infinite slowness in tiny runs and quick crouches, until she was behind a small buck who cropped incautiously, neither watchful for creeping danger, nor alert for unusual sound. She ended her successful stalk with a short run and a quiet bound that took the rabbit by surprise. He was hers and she ran, victorious, bolting for the tree, afraid to leave the pups alone too long.

She fed ravenously, lying outside the hole, strength coming back to her with each warm mouthful. Long before day dawned, wild and windy, she was curled again in the hollow, revelling as the small mouths tugged at her, and then, full-fed, the babies slept, cuddled against her, their tiny voices murmuring in whimpers that roused her from her half-sleep to lick each small head and savour it afresh.

The pups grew. As the days passed, they began to crawl over each other, their tiny voices strengthening as well as their limbs. Nan watched them, absorbed, and after each nightly forage, returned swiftly, licking eagerly at the faces that turned up to her, and settling comfortably, aware in every tingling nerve of the paws that thrust and pushed against her and of the greedy sucking mouths.

Each pup had its own character. The little bitch was boss, always ready to push her three brothers away and take all the nourishment for herself. She was, too, the first to greet Nan on her return home, and, as soon as her eyes opened and she could see as well as smell, she pushed her tiny body towards the large bulk that was her mother, and sought anxiously for the warm consoling lick from Nan's warm tongue.

Of the three little dogs, one was always second to the bitch, tumbling over himself in clownish antics designed to attract

Nan's attention, and noisy in his quick greeting when she returned from hunting. The other two were slower, and the littlest of all, the weakest, was timid, cowering away from his bullying brothers and sisters, always last to find his mother, and last to feed.

All of them were pure collie, for their father, although the shepherd did not know it, had been a dog from the farm beyond the hill that separated Nan's home from the lake. A dog called Moss, outstanding at the trials, with a pedigree boasting back to Hemp, supreme champion and ancestor of modern winning collies. It would have paid the shepherd handsomely to let Nan rear her pups. He could have asked a high price for them, fifty pounds each at least. It was as well he did not know.

Just now they were small and blunt-nosed, giving no sign of the breeding that was in them. Their patched black and white coats were clean, because Nan groomed them endlessly, but she herself was beginning to look rougher than usual, her coat tangled with burrs, her legs matted and muddy. No one would have guessed that she was a thoroughbred.

Ned Foley saw them one sunny day as he climbed the fells to sit and drink in the freedom of fresh air and sunshine, and the wide horizons. It was good to sit alone, in solitude broken only by the birds and running hares, instead of being trapped in the valley, where the house next door blocked the view, and people pressed all around him. Ned had once tramped the fells, doing odd jobs from Kendal to Penrith, and though he now lived a more civilized life, the old freedom still called him. The animal world was more real to him than his own, and had age not hindered him he would have returned to live in a rudimentary hut, alone on the windy fells, only the beasts for company.

The bitch had brought the pups into the sunshine, and, unaware of his presence, was playing with them as they rolled and tumbled over one another, growling in mock menace, biting in furious pretence of anger, grumbling and quarrelling in shrill yaps and whines and whimpers.

Ned cuddled into his thick navy coat, and pulled his well-loved, ragged old scarf more tightly round his neck. A smile added even more wrinkles to his old man's puck-face. Children loved Ned, trusting him on sight, aware of kindness in his dark eyes and his everlasting patience with all things, small or weak or ailing. There was a nip in the air, a hint of autumn and of frost to come, a murmuring anticipation of winter. He wondered how the bitch would fare when snow lay thick on the fells, and ice paralysed the running waters and the dark oily lake, and crusted the twiggy bushes and stunted trees with diamond-brilliant brittle frosted crystals.

He whistled, and Nan sat up at once, ears pricked, head alert, eyes searching for the source of the sound. He held out his hand, and she stared at him, and then growled a threat at her pups, chivvying them, hurrying them back to the hollow tree, out of his sight. When he approached the tree she met him with defiance, her ruff bristling, her teeth bared, snarling in anger.

He turned away at once, and left her, guessing at her story, aware that some violent emotion must have driven her away from the safety of her own home to rear her young on the bleak fells, where feeding was sparse, and danger hid in every hole and hollow.

That night Nan did not find food on the fells. The pups were demanding more from her than she had to give them, and she was desperate for nourishment. She left the four of them curled in the dry hollow of the old tree, and foraged farther and wider than before, until she caught the scent of man on the track that led to the village, lying in the fold under the hill, far below her.

Where there was man, there was also food, and she took the trail, following it, keen nose to the ground. She came to the stone wall surrounding the small garden of one of the more isolated cottages, and after a moment's hesitation, and a quick scenting of the air for danger, she jumped the wall, loosening a stone that fell with a small clatter on to the flagged path beneath the wall.

She waited, every muscle tense, but there was no sound from the sleeping cottage. Moonlight glinted dully on slate tiles, on a cluster of scented flowers that masked every other odour, and on the dustbin that stood against a ramshackle shed in a corner near the gate.

Nan knew about dustbins. She ran across the grass, a soundless shadow in the night. Her sharp nose edged up the lid, which fell, fortunately for her, in a well-dug flower bed, making no noise. She stood, her forepaws on the side of the bin, nosing inside, quick to distinguish every smell. The contents were out of her reach, the bin only partly filled, containing the end of a chicken carcase, and a large bone that gave off the enticing mouth-watering rich savour of roast meat.

She leaned her weight on the side and the bin crashed over, thundering on paved flags. She seized the bone, which was large and juicy. A man's voice raged at her through an open window. She leaped the wall and fled to the fells, where she found shelter under a dense low growing bush, and lay and worried savagely at her find.

There was marrow in the bone, and enough meat to ease the ache inside her. Not enough to feed her, or to deaden all cravings. She took the trail to the village again, making, this time, for the cottages lower down. Here there were better pickings, and the bins were fuller so that she had no need to overturn them. She browsed, undisturbed, on their contents, finding an end of a ham corner, bacon rinds, a half-empty tin of food, left for a farmyard cat, and then, unexpected bounty, in the corner of an old barn, bread and milk put out for the farm kittens, and, as yet, untouched.

Once a dog growled at her, sniffing angrily under the gap of a door. A cat swore, and aimed a clawed forepaw at her nose. She dodged aside, now well-fed, and anxious to return to her puppies. She had never left them for so long before, and uneasiness plagued her.

She sped up the hill, the stones rolling loose beneath her urgent paws. Tail and head and body in one sleek line, moon glinting on dirty black and white patched draggled fur and shining brilliant eyes, she reached the end of the man trail, and was on the uneven fells, floundering through boggy patch and over lichened ribs of bare rock, heading upwards, towards the hollow tree and her waiting pups.

They were big enough to wander. Eager, restive, full of life and fun, they came out of the hole and rolled and bit and pulled at tail and ear, noisy and heedless, unaware of any danger that might threaten them.

The little bitch was strong enough to walk some distance away from the hollow tree. She stared at the moon, astounded by the glow in the sky, and shivered when the wind swished the long grass that hid her from her brothers. Her small nose was aware of scent, unidentifiable, sometimes exciting, sometimes frightening. She crouched in the grass, instinct telling her to hide, although she did not know why. The grass was dew-wet, jungle thick, and blocked all vision. High above her, ears of seeded rye quivered in the wind.

The cruising owl did not see the little bitch. She was too well hidden. But the seeking eyes saw the three tiny dogs rolling and fighting, and before any of them knew what had happened, a giant shape dropped out of the sky, soft feathered, and took the smallest pup in its groping talons, and flew off, hooting in triumph.

The tiny bitch heard her brother's shrill terrified squeal. The owl flew low over her head, the pup held tight in its claws. She cowered, quivering with terror, too frightened to move. The two remaining dog puppies crept back to the sheltering darkness and trembled together, and dozed, to dream of a noiseless shape that dropped from the night, and woke, whimpering, to huddle even closer against each other for warmth and safety.

Nan, running over uneven ground, hauling herself desperately up the terraced ridges, heard the pup's shrill call, and found new strength in panic. She raced to the hollow, and searched inside, finding only two puppies. They rushed to her, small paws frantic against her face as they stood on hind legs, whimpering their horror and their greetings together.

She licked each face swiftly, nosed the dry leaves, and then searched the ground beyond the tree, finding the scent where the pups had played. And then nothing. She sat and keened to the arched uncaring sky.

The little bitch heard her and whimpered. Nan's ears pricked. A moment later she was nosing the ground. This time she found the trace left by her pup, moving in an unerring line through the dense overhanging grass, until she found the trembling tiny bitch who greeted her with frantic fervour. Nan lifted her gently in butter-soft jaws.

The two dog puppies welcomed their sister with grunts and squeals and tiny nips from their new sharp teeth, and the four animals curled tightly together, the pups still shaking with fear. Nan lay desolate, mourning her lost baby. Long after the little ones slept, she stretched out, her nose on her paws. Her wide eyes stared at the grass-covered opening beyond which the night was eclipsed by a shadowy dawn that brightened to an overcast silver-hued day.

CHAPTER TWO

THE big, steamy, old-fashioned room at the *Swan* was filled with men and with pipe-smoke; with noise and with laughter; with bragging and betting. Hounds and sheepdogs sprawled spatchcock on the flagged stone floor, opening suspicious eyes to stare at each other, to growl a warning, and then lapse, exhausted, into sleep. It had been a long hard day.

The sheepdogs were always tired out after their work on the fells, where men and dogs tramped relentless miles in all weathers, checking the beasts for signs of footrot, or maggot, or any of the other multitudinous ills that bedevilled the flocks. Today their masters relaxed beside the men who had been lucky enough to steal hours from work and follow the Hunt.

The first fox of the year had been flushed from cover in Sleepy Hollow, had run through a culvert, and then turned at right angles to plunge into dense undercover in Seven Acre Wood. From here he had come into the open, showing himself on the fells, before hurtling, breakneck, through tussocky heather, and vanishing with a last derisive wave of his copper brush into a rocky earth from which he disappeared completely.

The men and hounds were left to tramp through rain that drenched their clothes and damped their spirits, back to the warmth and familiar comfort of the *Swan* and the first Hunt Tea of the season.

Sated with ham and tongue and sausage rolls, with apple pie and cream, with home-baked wholemeal bread and salty farm butter and damson jam, the men were drowsy, comfortable at last. Men from Horton, and from beyond Horton

Mere, from Buttonskille, and from Bruton-under-the-Water, all congregated to talk of the day's events, of the performance of individual hounds, of the sly cunning of the fox, and of the red hunter's many misdeeds.

Wet clothes steamed, the steam mingling with the rank smoke of blackened pipes. Logs crackled in the wide brick fireplace, slipping now and then with a sputter of flame and a sifting of fine ash. Flames reflected on glinting china jugs that hung from the well-oiled beams, and sparkled and shone on the willow pattern plates that decorated the old black dresser.

Voices grumbled about the weather, which had put paid to one of the heaviest harvests for several years. Wheat and barley lay in tangled desolation in the sodden fields. The river Brue, which dropped over rocky crags before it made its chuckling way into Horton Mere, had twice poured over its banks and flooded Buttonskille. Acres of disappointment lay outside the *Swan*.

'Makes you wonder what you done to deserve it,' an unidentified voice said mournfully from the far side of the room. Heads nodded soberly in agreement. Mrs. Jones, the landlady, her round face serious, poured mild or bitter as the requests reached her, saying nothing, watching all of them, sharing their dejection.

Pete Lanark, the sheepfarmer from Five Ways, had other thoughts on his mind. He was a lean, angular heavy-jawed man, his beard always blue on his chin no matter when he shaved, his dark eyes watchful under thick wiry brows, with hair that was a wire thatch too, never lying sleek to the comb. He moved easily, and boasted a tireless walk that covered miles of fells daily; his talk was always of sheep and of dogs, his thoughts on the sheepdog trials at which his little bitch, Bet, often took high honours.

'Train anything . . . and win with it,' he repeated stubbornly, a little too much beer temporarily in control of tongue and brain. He banged his mug on the table and called to Mrs. Jones for another half pint to speed him on his road.

'Train anything?' Ned Foley's wrinkled mischievous puck face broke into a sudden grin. 'Try a greyhound then, for rounding up your sheep, or one of those daft overbred

17

poodles that town women fancy. Little coat and Wellington boots and all.'

Ned's creased brown face continued to grin, as he thought of a dog he had seen in Kendal not so long back. Dressed up like a little doll, in coat and boots and a jewelled collar, with the poor brute looking sheepish and yearning for a romp in the mud and a roll in a cowpat, and a chase through the heather ending in the blood of a rabbit hot in its jaws. No accounting for the whims of town folk.

Ned could sympathize with pampered creatures, remembering his own free days, his wild days, his tramp days, before age and circumstance civilized him and reduced him to living in a good brick house where he felt caged and confined. He still roamed the hills, knowing the fells and the woods and the becks and the tarns as well as he knew his own shadow. He could also, if he would, tell a man where the fox lay hid, where otters splashed in the flooding dawnlight, where salmon dreamed in the summer sun, lying just beneath the water, basking in rare warmth.

'Train anything in the sheepdog line,' Pete said hastily, caution reasserting itself. 'Don't matter what – give me a dog with a strong eye and a willing heart and I'll teach him. Come down gentle as a feather on the sheep – like old Bet here.'

Bet, hearing her name, wagged an appreciative tail, settled her black nose on her two white forepaws and slept, dreaming of rabbits that sat and waited for her to catch them. A leg twitched and her tail thudded and Pete laughed.

'Train anything,' he repeated.

'Like to bet?' Ned asked, always willing, as were all the men, to bet on the outcome of a Hunt, the winner at a Show or a Trial, and even the chance of a fine day come next Sunday week.

Pete grinned, his long, full-lipped mouth quirked and wry.

'I'll bet you a fiver to a mug of ale that you can't bring me a sheepdog I can't train to my own satisfaction,' he said.

'Done.' Ned lifted his foaming mug and drank to the bargain, knowing Pete would regret it in the sober light of the next day, knowing where to find a pup that would challenge all sanity in the teaching, knowing that the money was already his. He grinned again, his dark eyes glinting with amusement.

Pete whistled his bitch, and she followed him eagerly, as unaware as her master of the sufferings that were to be theirs in the years to come.

Ned, left alone, gazed thoughtfully into his beer mug, and plotted carefully. He hugged the thought of an easily won fiver, happily ignorant of the fact that even his cunning was to be severely tested, and his schemes foiled for some time by the obstinate determination of a little sheepdog bitch, at that moment living free, high on the fells.

CHAPTER THREE

NED was intrigued by the little family hidden on the moors. He often watched the pups playing. He saw their first stumbling steps strengthen and change to a speedy rolling puppy gait, and their games become fiercer, as they snapped and snarled and fought in tussles that were half fun and half earnest, practising for a life that might well be rougher and wilder than that of most dogs.

Nan hunted, sometimes by day, but more often, fox-like, during the dusky hours before darkness was complete. There were few people about at that time, and she felt that men threatened her safety. Man destroyed her young.

She did not feed well. The bins she raided were often moved, so that they were inside a shed, out of reach, or had the lids tied securely. No one liked being wakened by the sound of crashing. One night, returning to a source of frequent bones, she met pepper for the first time, and retreated, sneezing violently, her eyes watering and smarting. Blinded, she hid beneath a thick laurel bush and remained there for ten minutes, rubbing her paws forlornly over first one eye and then the other, to remove the inexplicable pain. After that, she left the bins alone.

Hunting was not easy. Sometimes she caught rabbits, but they were few and wary and she had not enough speed to catch hares. Sometimes she found part of a fox's kill; at others she stalked smaller prey, and she discovered that the ricks on the outlying farms always sheltered rats. She learned to lurk and pounce and kill, shaking the rat brutally to make sure it was dead and could not harm her when she let it go.

Most of the farms also kept cats, and there was often a bowl of bread and milk left in the yard, and on two occasions she found the half eaten carcases of chickens that had died mysteriously and been given to the cats to tear.

It was time for her pups to be weaned, and she began carrying the kill home to them, letting them worry and fight and snarl over part of a rat or a rabbit, learning to feed on solid food, and learning the smell of their prey.

Ned, seeing tell-tale bones round the tree, tried to entice the pups with his own offerings, but Nan had instilled fear into them, and they remained wary, knowing that if their mother came by when the man was there she would chase them back to safety, and use her sharp teeth to nip viciously and ram the lesson home. When he had gone, they crept out and attacked the food ravenously, and even Nan sometimes satisfied her hunger with his gifts of horsemeat or of part of stillborn calf, begged from a farmer to help feed Ned's own dog and cat and the pet foxcub that played with both animals and lived free in his yard, convinced that it too was a domestic beast. He had found it in a deserted earth after the Hunt had killed the vixen.

As he watched the pups grow he thought more and more of the wager he had made with Pete. The biggest was a fine sturdy little beast, his puppy features sharpening as he grew, his brown eyes clear and intelligent. He was frisky with youth, and more lively than the other two, often romping by himself. He would chase absurdly after a butterfly, or pounce and worry a piece of torn fur, then hunt for stones which he carried in his mouth and later abandoned, looking at them with a wagging tail and questioning eyes as if wondering why they did not move, as other things did.

He became used to seeing Ned there, and did not bother about the man so long as he did not move towards him. Should Ned hold out a hand, the pup backed away, growling. Ned grinned. He had all the time in the world, and was sure of his own powers. He would soon tame the little animal.

He took care that Nan never saw him, but the bitch was wary, for the scent of man lay strong on the ground, and often the tell-tale of his old pipe stopped her as she came down the hillside towards her home. She always waited until he had gone, and then circled the tree uneasily, summoning the pups, who came to her and greeted her ecstatically, each one vying to attract her attention. They stood on their hind paws, scrabbling against her sides, lifting their small faces until they were level with their mother's, eager to be first for the swift warm caress of her loving tongue. Only when this ritual was completed did they look for food.

Ned watched them from a distance. One day he brought a toy with him, a piece of frayed old rope, that all his own dogs had loved. He left it near the tree. Inquisitive, the biggest pup came to look. He sniffed the rope, which smelled of many things; of strange dogs and of dust and chicken food and Ned and tar and oil. He backed away, growling, as his brother and sister came to see what had attracted him.

He touched the rope gently, using an inquisitive paw. The rope did not move. It lay in front of him, inert, lifeless, smelling strange, but apparently harmless. Experimentally, he gripped it in his teeth and it twisted on the ground.

All three pups backed away from it, snarling. Nan was hunting, and had left them to search higher on the fells, desperate for food for herself and her family. The young appetites were growing as rapidly as the small rotund bodies.

The biggest dog puppy pounced suddenly, now certain that the strange object held no threat in it. He shook it and it wriggled enticingly, so that his brother and sister each grabbed part of it and pulled, the rope twisting between them as if it was alive. They dropped it, bounded away, bouncingly, not yet in full control of their muscles, mocked it, snapping, barked at it, daring it to move away from them, and then thrust each other out of the way in a wild attempt to grab the new toy and keep it, each for himself.

The big dog puppy pulled the rope end, and began to run. His smaller brother gripped it in the middle, and, surprisingly, was rolled over and dragged for a few inches, his expression astounded, so that Ned grinned to himself, well pleased at the success of his game. He left them to play, and also left them a hunk of meat, part of a rabbit, the fur still attached. The sheepdog was unexpectedly useful, as he could give her the remains of his own illicit meals, and no one would ever find the skins and ask questions, or if they did, would assume that the little bitch was eating her own kill.

When he came back next day the rope was still occupying the puppies' games. They were so engrossed that they did not see the man approach. The bigger dog puppy dropped his end, and braced himself to run and pounce and grab it again, and at that moment Ned reached out his gloved hand and picked him up.

Startled, the little beast growled frantic defiance, and the other two, seeing their brother seized in a giant hand and held high, kicking, squealing, and squirming, bolted for shelter, and crouched inside the tree panting.

Ned dropped the little beast into a sack. The pup quivered in terror, smelling a mixture of fox and cat and dog, for all of them had slept on the sack at times. It smelled also of mud and dust and petrol, of chicken feed and potatoes. It was dirty and stifling, and the stench was overpowering, so that the small creature quivered in fear, and, when Ned at last released him on the mud floor of his garden shed, cowered away from the man, too bemused to show even a token of defiance. The jolting journey down the fellside had been filled with a multitude of unknown terrors.

Ned looked at his new acquisition. There were unmistakable signs of collie breeding. The sleek coat was mainly black, but the pup had a large white triangular patch between his forelegs, his mother's white left forepaw, and a patched blotch of white over one eye, which gave him an oddly rakish look. He sat in his corner, and stared at the man, flopears pricked, expression wary.

Ned brought a tin dish in which he mixed minced meat and brown bread, all of it well soaked in blood from a piece of liver. The pup's nose twitched and his mouth watered. He was always hungry. But he made no move to feed until the man left him alone in the strange darkness of the unfamiliar shed, among unidentifiable bewildering smells from paint, and varnish, and oil, and an empty petrol can, and from paraffin in another can; from the chicken feed in a sack in the corner, the potatoes under the rough wooden work bench, and over all the choking reek of smoke that poured constantly from the rank old pipe that was seldom out of

23

Ned's mouth, tobacco being his present compensation for his housebound state.

The pup fed. He was lonely for his brother and sister, and for his mother. He was in a vast place that was high and dark and cold and bleak, and filled with menace. He nosed forlornly over the ground, looking for a place that was small and friendly and secret, in which he could curl and hide.

Finally he crept into a cranny between the potato bag and the wall, where he could feel, instead of the warm yielding fur of the other pups, the hard thrust of cold sacking. He lay with his head on his paws and whimpered bitterly, alone for the first time in his short life, and hating the loneliness.

A few minutes later Ned returned. He brought a small cardboard box, on the bottom of which he had put a rubber hot-water bottle, covered with two layers of thick blanket, borrowed from the cat. This would make a warm and comfortable bed, and in time the pup would become accustomed to being alone. Ned was not sure whether to introduce him to his three animals and start training the dog himself, or to hand him straight over to Pete, who might prefer to use his own methods on the little beast.

As the door opened, spilling light across the floor, the pup pressed himself, quivering, against the wooden wall of the shed. He stared forlornly at the tremendous boots and massive legs that made the floor vibrate. It was some minutes before Ned found him, and when he did so, and put his hand down to grab the small body, the little dog snapped and bit, drawing blood.

'More fool me,' Ned said ruefully. The small teeth were sharp. The pup must be all of twelve weeks old.

The man returned to the house, for his falconer's glove. He had once tamed a falcon, and used it to poach for him. It was more certain than any other method, and quieter than a gun, and easy enough to explain that he was merely exercising the bird and had not known that it would fly at a rabbit or young hare. It was time he found another. There was a challenge in falconry that he enjoyed, and he also enjoyed the trust of the bird, and the satisfying knowledge that it would fly into the wide sweep of sky and choose to come

24

back to him, of its own free will, rather than escape to freedom.

The pup had not moved. Ned lifted him gently, and put him in the box. He resisted at first, bracing himself, climbing out on to the floor again, away from the strangely alarming stench of cat that made the tiny ruff on his neck bristle, and caused him to growl.

Ned lifted the collie into the box, pressing a hand on his back. He stroked the soft fur on his head. There was an obscure comfort in the hand, but the pup was not friendly, nor would he accept the comfort. He remained tense, every muscle hard and unyielding, anxious only to escape, and find his way back to the hollow tree that was home, to the warm companionship of his brother and sister, and to his mother's warm caresses.

Ned left him, and shut the door. The little beast was full fed; slowly, the warmth of the hot-water bottle penetrated the blankets. He relaxed, no longer cold, but still desperately alone. He curled himself into a tight little ball, and dozed, and waked, and whimpered.

Up on the fellside, Nan returned to the hollow tree, proud with success, carrying a young rabbit in her jaws. It was dead, but untouched, and she dropped it by the hole and barked. The two pups crept towards her, remembering the man, afraid that he might still be there and pounce and lift them too, sky-high and squealing, and then stride away over the moors. All the pups were intelligent. Memory was vivid, and no lesson needed teaching twice.

Nan was puzzled. The third pup was missing. She ran hastily into the tree, but he was not there. She cast about on the hillside. His track vanished near the rope, the rope that smelled of her pups, and also of many things that she associated with man. It also reeked of the man who brought food to them, and who so often sat and watched them.

She pushed the pups into the hollow tree, and brought them the rabbit. Soon hunger overcame the remnants of fear, and they began to feed. Nan ran down the hillside, towards the village.

The world had lost its identity, the objects in it no longer sharp, but blurred and indistinct with dusk. She relied on her nose to guide her, and Ned's trail was clear, as immediate as if it had just been laid, for his boots stank of chickens. Before going out on to the fells and taking the pup he had collected the eggs and cleaned out his hen house.

In the village below, the dark sharp shadows of houses, etched against a dimming sky, were patched with brilliant light. Lights meant people, and Nan lay under a bush waiting until all was dark and still. She was patient and determined. So had she often lain guarding the sheep, or watching over a new-born lamb while the shepherd attended to the mother. Time was meaningless.

An owl called, long and low and mournful, looming above her, too close both in sight and scent; a weasel slid from a cranny in a wall, and slipped along the ditch. Nan had no interest. She was waiting for darkness, when men would cease to walk the streets, and she could have peace in which to find her pup, safe from interference. Her months in the wild had made her cunning, and she had learned many things.

When she foraged among the dustbins men had yelled at her, thrown bottles and stones at her, and fired shotguns at her. She had no intention of having anything to do with any of them. Her own master beat her when she annoyed him. The sight of a stick was enough to send her cringing against the nearest wall, abject at the thought of the pain that it would inflict. When the shepherd walked on the fells she kept well out of range of his crook, and gave him instant obedience, lest that too thrashed down upon her back.

The last lights were dying. A man, late home, called good night to a friend. A gate creaked. Footsteps thumped along the path. A key scraped in a lock. A door slammed.

Silence.

Then only the wind in the grass, the soft slip of footsteps from a passing cat. Nan bristled and growled under her breath. The cat was seeking the source of a rumour borne on the breeze, the whisper of a pretty tabby, ripe for his attentions, and he had no time for dogs. He passed by, unheeding, attentive only to the exciting summons, to the enticement and the fascinating allure that called him urgently,

26

the faraway sounds unheard by any but feline ears, the scent that was for his nose only.

A sheep bleated. Cows lowed in a distant field. A train rattled through the night and sounded its horn in derisory greeting to the sluggard sleepers. These were familiar noises, and none of them hinted danger.

The collie stretched herself, stiff from waiting. She found the trail again, skirted the garden, and jumped the wall into the yard. Nose to ground, she found a confusion of scent, for Ned had walked over and around his yard time after time, and nowhere could she find a trace of the pup.

Until he whimpered.

It was the faintest sound, a ghost of a cry, faint from exhaustion, the last complaining wail before he fell into a sleep so deep that nothing would wake him, until day restored him and hunger whipped him to life.

Nan stiffened, instantly alert, head cocked, ears pricked, eyes wide, listening.

The sound did not come again, but she knew she had not been mistaken. Her pup was near. She moved quietly, her ears flicking backwards and forwards to trap the tiniest murmur.

It came again, a forlorn baby noise, full of desolation.

Nan ran to the shed, now certain. She whined, a mere trickle of noise. The pup heard. He lifted his head, immediately awake, and answered her, hope intensifying his cries. Nan called back, and he was out of the box, and behind the door, sniffing under the crack, whimpering frantically. The bitch whined back at him, and he basked in the wonderful reassuring scent of her, the memory of her warmth and comforting bulk, and began to yelp, and then to bark at her. It was his first real bark, and for a moment, it startled him to silence.

Nan growled.

Noise was dangerous, though had she known it, there was no need to fear. Ned was high on the fells, on his own ploys, and there was no one close enough to hear her.

There was earth under the door, plainly visible in the dappling moonlight.

The collie began to dig. Her paws scraped at the ground, flinging the dry soil away behind her, working with desperate speed. The pup was soon able to see through the crack, to see her earth-covered nose and busy paws, and suddenly realizing what she was doing, he tried to help, but his tiny claws and pads slipped hopelessly on the hard-packed soil, and he gave up, and sat and whined encouragement and pleading.

By the time the moon had slipped up the sky to shed light across the yard and filter uncannily into the crack and through the cobwebby dust-thick window, the hole was big enough for the pup to slip under the door, easing his small body with frantic haste. Long before he had time to reach her Nan had grabbed him by the scruff of his neck and was pulling him towards her.

He was plump, and the hole was not quite large enough for easy progress. He stuck, just at the edge of the door. Nan braced her forepaws and her shoulders and tugged, and he came through so suddenly that she overbalanced, but she never let him go.

It was quiet under the moon. The soft background grumble of roosting chickens was the only sound that accompanied the reunion of mother and son. For a few moments they were heedless, the pup jumping at her, licking at her face and missing time and again, and she licked his smooth warm body as if she would wash it away.

A lorry thundered through the village street, changing gear with a shuddering roar as it cornered on the sharp bend, and faced the steep hill that led back to the main road. The noise alarmed the bitch.

Unceremoniously she grabbed her pup by the scruff of his neck and began the journey home. He was no longer small enough for her to find it easy to carry him. He was plump and solid, and although at first he co-operated, hanging quietly from her jaws, once they were on the fells he began to struggle, wanting to run himself, and not be carried so uncomfortably and ignominiously.

Soon she had to drop him. She snapped at him irritably when he tried to run, and he lay beside her, while she regained her breath and gathered her strength. It was a long, slow journey home. She would not let him walk, but it was necessary to stop frequently.

Once they drank from a trickling rill that rippled over slimy rock to join the brook. The pup watched the moon-specked water glitter mysteriously as it thrust against rocks that littered the bed. He would have liked to stop and play, to run into the shimmering shallows and splash his paws. He loved water. It fascinated him, breaking away from beneath him, unlike the solid unyielding ground.

Nan picked him up again, for the last lap of the journey. She was desperately tired. She had not fed before starting on her search, and the three months of motherhood had drained some of her strength. Soon the pups would be old enough to fend for themselves and she would not feel the tie that bound them to her, but that was in the future. She plodded on.

Her slow paws paddled over low-lying ground where bog-moss held water in its spongy depths, and her legs were soaked. The first real frost of the season lay on the air. The ground was cold, and long before she reached the tree she was shivering.

The two pups heard her coming and ran to greet her. She licked them, a perfunctory acknowledgement, and dropped their brother on to the dry leaves, and crawled in beside him. They came too, and curled to sleep, her newly rescued son pushing hard against her, as if to ensure that she never left him again. Even when he slept, the memory of the after-noon troubled his dreams, and he whimpered and woke, and reached out his blunt nose to reassure himself. Each time the bitch was swift to lick him.

It took time for her to recover. When she did she found the remains of the rabbit, and slipped outside the hollow tree to feed. The pup found her gone, and, whining abjectly, came to look for her, so that she finished her meal with him curled up against her, his tiny head across her hind paws, his small legs kicking at her as he dreamed.

When she had stilled her hunger she lifted him and took him inside, and he did not even wake. Contentedly, she slept with the pups, her sleep so profound that she did not scent the weasel that fed on the stripped bones of the rabbit, lying outside their hiding place.

Ned returned to his home at daybreak with a guddled trout tucked under his coat. He went to the shed, saw the hole beneath the door and whistled. At first he wondered if one of his own animals had tried to get at the pup, but soon realized that the bitch had come to claim her son. He shook his head, smiling and, feeling that she deserved to keep him with her after showing so much devotion, decided that Pete would have to wait.

Winter was coming. It would be a brutal season, out on the fells, and the collie would need better shelter than that to be found in the old tree, or her pups would die. The little beast would be his yet, and he coveted it, half wondering if he would not keep it and blow the wager. Yet it was a pity to waste a sheepdog. The breed did not make good pets.

He blew on his frozen hands and went inside to grill his trout. The boisterous welcome of his own dog and the young fox made up for his loss. There was plenty of time. Time meant no more to Ned than it did to the sheepdog. And, meanwhile, the trout was good.

CHAPTER FOUR

The pups began to learn. There were trails to follow, nose down, high on the fells. The track of rabbit, of hare, of mouse; bird scent from the partridges; danger scent to be avoided, of stoat and fox and weasel.

It was not easy for the bitch. Unlike the ranging foxes, she had centuries of domestication behind her. The vixen could show her cubs the ways of the fells, ways she had learned from her own mother, and that her mother too had learned, as a cub. Nan had to teach herself as well as her pups.

Nor were the pups as fleet as foxcubs, though their speed would increase as they grew. They lacked the wild beast instinct to freeze at danger, or run swiftly away, although they soon learned to creep into the hollow tree at unfamiliar sounds or smells.

Winter soon would follow on the heels of darkening autumn. Leaves lay thick in the woods, and the pups had ample warning of passing strangers. No man but Ned had, as yet, glimpsed them, though many of the shepherds had seen Nan, and known from her filthy matted fur and gaunt appearance, that she must be running wild. She gave none of them a chance to catch her.

The pups learned to recognize the sound of the Hunt. They hid from the flying pack, and only came out when men and beasts had gone from the hills. Nan hunted for them, and brought small live mice for them to kill by themselves.

The nights were colder. They huddled together for warmth in the tree, and, when they ventured out in the dawning, watched, bright-eyed and intrigued, the small white puffs of breath that came from each mouth. They walked warily on frost-grey grass, which struck bitter chill at their pads.

All the pups were more venturesome now. One bright morning, when the sun splashed light over the fells, and dark cloud-shadows chased mysteriously across the ground, the bigger dog climbed the little hill that peaked sharply beyond the tree.

He was sixteen weeks old, and full of curiosity. He was matted and dirty, and though healthy, was now far too thin. Nan had not solved the problem of feeding all four of them well.

Beyond him, on the skyline, was an old ewe, wandering in search of better feeding than usual. She cropped the grass steadily, a lean beast, her winter wool not fully grown. The pup caught her scent.

He turned, sniffing the wind. It was a new smell to him, exciting and strangely familiar, all in one. The ewe lifted her head and saw him, and turned away, bleating.

The pup ran. This was something no one had told him about, something that he had to do, an urge that was deeper than any that motivated him. He did not need teaching. Tail and head and body in perfect line, he crept behind the sheep and began to stalk her, his eyes fierce with delight, glowing, hypnotic. Against her will she began to walk, keeping away from him, moving slowly, aware that here was one of the dogs that herded her, and that he was willing her to obey, and driving her where he pleased.

He shifted suddenly, running behind her, turning her, pushing her, yet never near enough to touch her. He dropped to the ground when she began to trot, instinct guiding him, and, as she resumed a more leisurely pace, he crept behind her, not knowing where he wished to drive her, yet knowing that drive her he must.

He spent some time amusing himself, eagerly busy, and then the shepherd's dog came running, looking for the stray, barked angrily at the intruder, and drove the ewe back to join her sisters. Foiled, the pup sat and panted at the sun, forgetting, now that the sheep was gone, all the instincts that had recently mastered him.

He did not remember the sheep until some weeks later, by

which time he was a sleeker animal, half-grown, and savage, ready to bite any creature that threatened him, ready to snap and snarl at man. It would be a puzzle for Ned to catch him now.

The autumn winds were blustering over the fells, sleeking the almost leafless trees, streaking the heather, bending long grass in rippling waves. Nan and the other pups were hunting, but the biggest stayed by himself, aware of a need to be alone and work out an urge that had bothered him intermittently for days.

Ecstasy came to the dog, alone on the rolling fell, alone in a demented world, a world of vivid scent that packed the flying wind, a place of swirling cloud that shadowed the ground, scudding under his inquisitive nose, bothering him with sudden dark and light on the springy grass. A place of speeding heedless rushing air that rumpled his coat and bristled his ruff and sent him wild with heady inexplicable excitement.

He circled, chasing his tail, dangling idiotically just out of his reach. He widened his circle, forgetting the chase, and head and body and tail flowed into smoothness, all in line, and his eyes focused on a group of grey rocks, huddled among the spilling patches of fading purple heather.

He was a grown dog, a sheepdog, making the flock obey him. Generations of ancestors told him what to do. His eye on a raddled boulder, he crept to it, defied it, quelled it to obedience, and then, pup-like, forgot his task, and sat with the wind in his fur, his head raised, and his panting mouth a-laugh, wide open, sucking in gulps of ice-cold air. His tail, taking life of its own, weaved its own pattern of delight.

Before that week was ended he was looking for sheep, anxious to come upon them and herd them. There were many, scattered over the fells, grey moving hulks that caught his eye, or that advertised their presence on the wind that was never absent from the moors.

He derived endless pleasure from approaching them in a wide arc that brought them in front of him, and then, gently, persistently, pushed them before him, into the angle of a stone wall skirting a field, against a windbreak of shrubby trees, or into a fold in the ground.

He could not go unnoticed now.

One night, as wind blustered into the room every time the door was opened, Tom Ladyburn, the shepherd from Wellans', commented, as he drank at the *Swan*:

'Damn stray sheepdog pup up on the fells. Herded all the sheep for me and through a gap and out on to the hill. Had a devil of a time fetching them in again. Strayed all over the place.'

'Be worrying them next,' Ted Wellans said morosely. He was having family trouble, and it affected his temper. He was a big man, usually jovial, with the richest farm in the district, where he kept a herd of pedigree Jersey cows, and, as well, owned a fine flock of sheep. He lived in a fifteenth-century timbered farmhouse, a showplace, furnished with antiques that many a dealer between Kendal and Lancaster had seen and coveted.

'She's been up there on the fells half the summer and never worried sheep yet,' Ned Foley said.

'Wasn't a bitch. A young dog pup. Saw it streak for cover,' Tom Ladyburn lifted his brimming mug. 'Enough bother with dogs as it is.'

'Need bigger fines for sheep worrying,' the Huntsman, a small, brown-faced man with shrewd eyes volunteered. 'Heard that somewhere in the South they fine you two hundred pounds the first time your dog goes for sheep, and shoot it the second. Not many stray dogs round there.'

'Nobody'd stand for it here.' Jasper Ayepenny, the oldest man in the village, put a wrinkled hand down to stroke his bitch's warm muscular shoulder. Good old Nell, he thought. She'd never go for sheep. Getting old now, like him, and pretty nigh as rheumaticky. He sighed gustily, and then drank. No fun, being old. Took all day to do half a day's jobs, and soon have to sell the cows. Milking these nippy mornings was getting beyond him, and Bess Logan, with whom he lodged, was as unhandy as he, her arthritis keeping her almost permanently housebound.

'Have to do something about him.' Tom Ladyburn wiped his mouth with the back of his hand and settled his old check cap more comfortably, pulling it over one eye, giving his brown face a lean rakish look.

The old raftered room shook as wind flung itself against the walls. The log fire flared to flaming brilliance. The mocking blast roared in the chimney, startling the dogs into wakefulness as they lay beside their masters, patient, waiting for the word to go. The door of the *Swan* opened yet again, tore itself from the newcomer's hand and slammed shut.

'Sorry, Mrs. Jones.'

The landlady, about to remonstrate, flushed suddenly and swallowed her words, as a small plump man, his creased face pink and his dark eyes anxious, came into the light, shaking raindrops from his coat. Mr. Betwick, who owned the *Swan*, and the brewery as well. He nodded to the men, but his eyes sought out Ted Wellans, and he sat beside him, and called for a pint.

Conversations were resumed, and Ned Foley, in a corner beyond Jasper, debated the wisdom of telling of the sheepdog family up on the moors. Pete Lanark was in another corner of the room, arguing a price with a shepherd from Horton, who had come over to see if, by any chance, Pete had a ram for sale.

Outside the wind blustered, increasing to a high keening moan as it rattled doors and windows. Conversation lapsed, and the men took refuge in their old pipes, finding ease in the taste of tobacco, filling the room with the tang, uneasily aware of a curious atmosphere about the conversation between the brewer and Ted.

'Well, that's that, then.' Betwick did not sound satisfied. 'You can't do a thing?'

'How the hell can I?' Ted asked irritably. 'Can't talk to the kid nowadays. She won't even listen. Just flies into a tizz and slams out of the room.'

He shrugged himself into his coat, flicked his fingers at his Labrador dog, and marched past the men seated round the big scrubbed table, a tell-tale of angry colour on each cheek. The door slammed behind him. Only when his footsteps had died away did the brewer move. His 'Night, all' was curt. They heard his car start to urgent life, and roar away, the engine racing.

'What's all that about then?' Ned Foley asked, incorrigibly curious.

'Young Jim Betwick's taking out Sue Wellans. Reckon his dad don't like the way he drives that little red buzzer of his, or the time he comes home. Drives like a mad thing.'

'They all do.' Tom Ladyburn drained his mug and stood up, stooping to avoid the rafters. His sheepdog stretched, and nuzzled his hand. Tom sighed. 'Like my young Dick and his motor bike. He'll kill himself before he's through. Can't think of anything but speed. No caution built into the young. And no telling them either. Didn't want him to have it. But he's his own man now, so what can I do? No use talking.'

'That's the worst of it.' Jasper looked back on lads and girls he'd known who had flung themselves insanely to death. Jo Needler's boy, drowned in the lake, caught by the current where the river fed in, swimming in winter for a bet, and young Roger, who'd helped with the sheep at Wellans, and driven, hell-bent, into a wall, skidding one night, trying to beat his own record time home. And that bonny little lass down the end of the village, he'd forgotten her name, killed pillion-riding on her very first day in her new job. Took a lift home. 'You can't tell the young. You can't tell them anything.' He sighed again. No one ever listened to the old.

Tom Ladyburn went out, not wanting to gossip about his boss.

'Sue's a right pretty little lass, now,' the Huntsman said. He had known her since she was born, remembered her struggling behind them on her donkey, trying to keep up with the hounds, red in the face with temper because old Bridie never would go well and stopped, mulish, every half-mile.

'Young Jim's a wild one,' Pete Lanark said. 'Not like his dad. Too full of himself, and no time to be civil.'

'Thinks he's a ladykiller,' Mrs. Jones was acid, her memory suddenly stung into indiscretion as she recalled an incident a few months back. She regretted the remark as soon as she'd passed it, and poured another half pint for Ned Foley, her colour high and her lips tight, as if daring her tongue to utter another word.

The conversation drifted to other teenagers. The village had its share of them, but little trouble. There was always too much to do on the farms for any of them to have over much time to spare, and those who tended to make mischief went off to the towns and stayed there.

'Five minutes to go,' Mrs. Jones said.

There was swift emptying of mugs. The men buttoned their coats against the wind and the driving rain that drummed on the window panes.

Pete Lanark paused in the lane to speak to Ned.

'What about that pup you were going to get me?' he asked, half-joking, pulling up his collar against the downpour. 'Bet's almost eight now, and young Sam's going on four. Can't risk being left with only one dog, and if I get another I'll not have room for yours. Moira doesn't like dogs anyway, and she'd create if I had four.'

'I'll get him,' Ned promised. And he'd better too, he thought, if the pup was working by himself among the sheep up there on the fells. Somebody'd take a gun to him before long, and small blame to them.

'Within the next fortnight,' he promised, wondering if the promise was rash, knowing that time had hurried along faster than he'd realized and the pup would be half-grown and even less trusting.

Pete nodded, and went off towards his own farm, and Ned turned through the wind and stinging rain to his home, wondering how it was that Pete had ever married Moira, who was born and bred in a town, and hated all animals, and would not even have the young lambs inside to feed, like the other farm women.

Pete had built an outhouse for them, against the kitchen wall, warmed by the back of the big Aga. Luckily his two elder lads helped with the feeding bottles and Ned had visited one day and gone away grinning, for Bet, the sheep-dog, sat beside a leggy tottering lamb, with a cloth-wrapped bottle held firmly in her jaws. The lamb pulled and tugged at it, and the bitch showed every sign of absorbed enjoyment. When the bottle was empty she took it to Pete, who was feeding two more orphans on the other side of the room, went back to her charge and curled up beside it, licking its small black nose devotedly.

Ned piled wood on to his fire. He rarely bought fuel, but kept the flames fed with dead sticks salvaged from the fells,

37

and with dead wood brought in from the woods. He cleared only from the undergrowth, reckoning it helped the foresters and did no harm.

His cross-bred dog lay with its head across his feet. The fox climbed into the enormous armchair, the leather worn away with age, the stuffing overflowing from an ancient velvet cushion, and curled beside his master, head against his arm. The black cat climbed to his knee, and flexed her paws, clawing gently, her feet padding with every sign of satisfaction. Soon she leaned against Ned's thick woollen jersey, and, with half-closed eyes, began to lick the wool until a patch of it was sodden.

Ned stared into the flames, planning his campaign, aware that it would now need a deal of cunning to catch the pup.

CHAPTER FIVE

WINTER came early, bringing utter bleakness to the sodden moors on which rain had poured almost daily for weeks. Low-lying patches of ground were flooded, and even the drier places were slippery with wet. The bitch and her pups slid and floundered, and lay in damp misery in the tree. The smaller dog puppy, never as strong as the other two, weakened slowly. One dull morning, dragging behind the other three, he dropped to the ground, and, shivering, died. The bitch nosed his dead body unhappily, unable to understand why he did not move, and at last she left him, and followed the other two.

A straying fox, a-rage with winter hunger, found the puppy. He nosed the trail that the dogs had taken, and followed it to the hollow tree. From now, the pups were marked, and the raider knew where to come for them.

He came back nightly, but they were busy on their own hunts, and he found only the tantalizing traces that they had left behind them. Ill-fed on mice, he was determined to find the pups and take them. They were big enough to make a sizeable meal, but not big enough to endanger him if it came to fighting.

He met them at last at the point of time at which dusk meets darkness. They had been hunting near the village, and found a straying hen; and fed well. They came home incautiously, Nan distracted by the knowledge that a dog was in the vicinity. She had seen him twice, ranging on his own, a big rough cross-bred sheepdog-type animal, running wild, his own desires, at present, encompassing only the death of sheep for which he had insatiable appetite.

Nan, catching traces of his scent, sniffed eagerly, and not until they came close to the tree did she see the fox. By then, it was too late. He flung himself forward in a bounding pounce, grabbed the bitch puppy by the throat, and before he had twisted to fly down the hill, and seek cover for his meal, the pup was dead.

Nan chased him, desperate for her puppy, but she had no chance against the speed of the hardened killer. She returned to her last pup, and together the pair of them climbed the fell to a ruined shepherd's hut, where the roof over a half-fallen outhouse gave shelter from the weather.

Next day Nan left the pup and went off alone. The killer dog caught her scent on the wind, and determinedly tracked her down. They spent the day chasing one another through the soaked dead heather, in crazy games of tag, Nan never allowing him near her. The pup watched, bewildered, and then went off on his own, and herded Jasper's cows until the old man saw him, and yelled and threw a stone which failed to find a target.

That evening, as Pete Lanark was walking home with his sheepdogs, Bet and Sam, at his side, he looked down towards the village. Below him were the enclosed fields in which Ted Wellans kept his sheep, and running among them, biting and snapping, was one of the biggest sheepdogs he had ever seen. As he watched, the dog jumped for the throat of a frenzied ewe, and brought her down, bleating frantically, as he bit and tore savagely at her throat.

Pete began to run, yelling at the intruder, signalling to his own dogs, who raced towards the field and deployed, one on each side of it, ready to attack the killer. The killer did not wait. He was a coward, and knew himself outnumbered, and, as the dogs came towards him, he jumped the wall, and ran, coming close to Pete, who tried to trip him with his crook. The dog dodged away, and fled up the fell, where Nan joined him.

Pete called off his dogs, not wanting them hurt. He went to the dying ewe and hoisted her over his shoulder. No need to leave the carcase for the brute's return. Bet and Sam dropped to heel and followed quietly as he took the path that led to Tom Ladyburn's cottage. The dead beast would make a meal for a few folk anyway.

Tom swore when he saw the dead sheep.

'Get her to the butcher, I suppose,' he said wearily. 'We'll have to hunt those dogs out, or they'll feed all winter on the ewes and when lambing comes . . .'

'Too many damn stray dogs up here,' Pete answered irritably. Anger made him sick. A dog turned killer was far more messy and brutal in his vice than any fox.

'Too many everywhere. People won't take the trouble to keep them under control. Four thousand sheep a year killed by dogs. . . . A sight too many. We'll have to hunt that feller down.' Tom looked morosely at the still warm carcase of the dead sheep.

'There's a bitch running with him. We'll have to get them both.' Pete looked up the hill, but by now the darkness hid tree and ridge and hollow and only the swelling shape of Horton Pike loured black against the moon-dim star-pricked sky. 'Never catch them now.'

'We'll hunt them down tomorrow,' Tom said. He hefted the sheep. 'Put this away and put it out as bait. He'll be back, once he's found easy pickings. Once a killer, there's no cure. Coming to the *Swan*?'

Pete nodded, not being a man who wasted words. He waited while Tom huddled into his old coat, pulling the collar up and his cap peak down to cheat the chill of night. Beyond them the golden windows of the inn glowed a welcome, and their steps quickened, until at last they were pushing through the door to be greeted by the crow of ribald laughter that met one of the visiting cattle cake representative's seamier strokes of wit.

'That'll do,' Mrs. Jones said sharply, as she turned to smile at Tom Ladyburn and Pete.

'Look as if adder's ate all your eggs, you two,' said Jasper Ayepenny from his corner chair, and his red setter turned her gentle eyes away from solemn contemplation of her master's face to look at them, before dropping her head on to Jasper's knee. The old man's hand shook slightly as he stroked the silky fur.

'Killer dog killed one of Wellans' sheep,' said Tom, and Ted Wellans, hearing him, put down his beer mug with a heavy thump that jarred the table and sent rich shining droplets spattering.

41

'Have a care, Ted. Like spilling treasure.' Ned Foley remonstrated, and lifted his dog to lick the spilt drops.

'One of the best ewes, I'll bet,' Ted said wearily.

Tom nodded.

'The one with the ear that got torn on wire. Had twin rams last year. A good mother, too.'

'One thing goes wrong, the whole damn lot goes wrong.' Ted's voice was bitter.

'Never rains but it pours,' Jasper said, irritatingly trite, but agreeing with him.

'Have to get the dog.' The Huntsman, since his own cottage had been pulled down to make room for the motorway, lodged in the annexe of the *Swan,* and helped the landlady. He pulled beer for the two newcomers, knowing their tastes, and nodded as he rang up the cash on the register.

'Easier said than done,' Ted answered morosely.

'Dunno.' Tom emptied his glass slowly, savouring every drop, never stopping until it was empty. 'Kept the carcase of the sheep. We put that out tomorrow, and lie in wait. I reckon we'll get him before he knows what's hit him.'

'No use trying to chase him down?' asked one of the men from the nearby mining town, come visiting a cousin. Any excuse for a Hunt, no matter what the game.

'No use at all.' Pete was definite. 'We can put the carcase out at first light, and lie up then. Not too many of us. There's hedges round the field, and plenty of cover.'

'How many dogs? Just the one?' asked Ted, his mind only half on the sheep and the other half brooding irritably over his daughter's latest misdemeanour. One o'clock before she'd come home the night before, and she only seventeen, and never a word as to where she'd been or who with, though he'd a shrewd guess at the answer. And what the hell could he do with her? Couldn't put her over his knee, and couldn't talk to her either. And his wife as much at her wits' end as he was, and not knowing what to do and expecting him to work miracles. And now more bother, and that could snowball into a pack of trouble. One killer could put an end to dozens of sheep, once he'd got the taste of blood in his mouth. And more vicious than any fox.

'Two,' Pete answered. 'There was a smaller animal with him. A rough little thing, looked as if it had been living wild for weeks. Think it was a bitch.'

'She's been up there all summer, and never touched a single sheep,' Ned said, angrily and incautiously.

'A damn stray up there all summer and you knew, and you never told? Hang it all, Ned, you've no bloody sense.' Ted glared at him, his temper barely under control.

'Ned knows which animals are safe and which aren't,' the Huntsman's voice was placating. 'He's always up there watching. I've seen the bitch myself when I've been looking out the fox trails. Never seen her near the sheep.'

'She's been too busy with her pups.' Ned looked longingly at his empty glass, but he couldn't spare the price of another pint. He licked his lips longingly, and Pete saw the action and grinned, thinking how like an animal the little man was, with his love of the wild and his instinctive defence of its inhabitants. He looked like a thirsty fox. 'Have one on me, Ned.'

'If she's feeding pups she'll take anything,' Ted said glumly. 'Turns any bitch into a killer.'

'Not this one, she's too good with the sheep. She's a real sheepdog,' Ned answered. 'Loves sheep and protects them – I've watched her.'

'That'd be her pup herding my cows, I don't doubt. Tried to hit him wi' a stone, but he were too canny.' Jasper drained the last drop from his mug and beckoned to Nell, who stood beside him, waiting for him to lead the way from the room. It took him some minutes to rise from his chair, his mouth wry with pain. 'Damned rheumaticks nigh killing me,' he grumbled, and walked stiffly to the door. 'Night, all.'

The door swung shut behind him.

'Jasper's feeling his age. Aged pretty sudden, these last months,' Ned's eyes were on his dog, which sat bolt upright, ears a-cock, watching something behind a chair in the corner. 'Blow me, you've got mice, missus,' he said suddenly, and Mrs. Jones looked at the chair in horror.

'It's not a mouse.' Pete bent down, and then laughed. 'It's a frog, come in from the cold, I should think.' He picked it up, holding it firmly, squeezing the slippery body, as the kicking legs thrashed futilely, and took it outside and dropped it in the ditch. Disappointed, Ned's dog dropped to the ground, ears flopping again.

'Never know what you'll find next, in here,' the Huntsman said, as he gathered the empty mugs and glasses on to a tray. 'I leave the door wide to air the place each morning, and practically anything's likely to come inside. Cats, kittens, dogs. Even had a young pig in one day.'

'Never saw anything like it,' Mrs. Jones said, laughing, her plump face vividly amused. 'Pig running one way squealing, and Huntsman on his tail wi' the broom, shooing and shouting, and chairs upset and a crash against the table, and Huntsman full length on the floor, pig between his legs, and bucket of soapy water flying across the room. Took us half an hour to get rid of the beast and a couple of hours to put things straight.'

'And you didn't laugh then, and neither did I,' the Huntsman said. 'Cor, that was a day. Get cockerels and hens in too and even a hedgehog, pinching the cat's milk.'

'What about those dogs?' Ted asked, having heard none of the conversation, his own thoughts going round and round in his head like a mallard on a dew pond.

'We'll get them,' Pete promised. 'I'll bring my shotgun, and if one or two more will come too . . .'

'You're not going to shoot the bitch?' Ned said desperately, feeling for her as if she were his own, for all his failure to gain her trust.

'She may not come with the dog,' Tom said appeasingly, knowing that she almost certainly would, and that if she did she had to die too, for ten to one she'd taste the sheep, and living wild like that, who knew what lifelong habits would be broken?

'Leave me the pup. I'll catch him and keep him,' Ned said, almost pleading, wanting to save the pup more than he wanted anything.

Pete looked at the old man suspiciously.

'Would that be the sheepdog you were promising me?' he asked. 'Bred on the fells, and never handled at all? What kind of bet is that?'

'You said you could train anything,' Ned answered. 'And

if you won't have him, I will. But you'd be missing something. He's a natural with the sheep. Streaks round them and herds them as if he'd been doing it for years. And never a flurry or a panic. A quiet walk down, and the pup behind them, everything under control.'

'I dunno.' Pete rubbed his chin, thoughtfully, the stubble harsh against his hand. 'A pup that's never been handled . . . how old would he be?'

'About three or four months,' Ned said, purposely pretending ignorance.

'And savage. He'll never trust men, or be responsive. Need to handle a puppy almost from birth.'

'He'll be a dead loss, Ned,' Tom Ladyburn fondled his own sheepdog's head. The long tail beat approvingly on the floor, and the dog licked his master's hand. 'He'd best be shot too.'

A log slithered in the fireplace. The shining copper kettle, always on the hob, puffed steam into the silent room. All other conversation had lapsed, as the men listened to the argument. The big clock in the corner ticked hurriedly, its swinging pendulum flashing reflected flame from the fire. A dog grunted in its sleep. Another sighed deeply.

'Let me have him,' Ned repeated obstinately. 'I've trained a twelve week fox, haven't I? He was fierce as a tiger cub when I took him. And even the otter I had was tame enough and he wasn't a young 'un.'

'And he bit the postman,' the Huntsman reminded him.

'Postman was scared and kicked out at him, and the otter knew. Animals always know when you're scared. Seen a dog bark at a frightened child when he's a softie with everyone else. Can't understand the smell of fear. It upsets them.'

'Like my Johnny,' Pete said. Johnny was his five-year-old son, born when the other three children were all in their teens. 'Johnny's never scared of any animal and frightens the living daylight out of me sometimes. Put his arm round a swan's neck, and he a cob guarding the pen. And the bird never harmed him.'

'Had to turn him out of the Emperor's stall before now,' Tom Ladyburn said. 'Passed there the other day and there was Johnny sitting on the half-door, babbling away to the

45

bull, and him so naughty we can't handle him alone. Takes Rob and me and a pitchfork to watch the old brute. Not like Majesty. Now that was a gentle beast. But nothing scares young Johnny – or not in the beast line, anyway. He used to love Majesty. Talk to him by the hour.'

The men nodded, remembering Majesty, who had been slaughtered when Ted's prize cow contracted foot and mouth, a year or so before.

'Then the pup's mine,' Ned said, his expression relieved, and, before any of them could contradict him or argue further, he and his dog were gone from the room, and only the swinging door was left to show that they had been there at all.

'Did we say it was?' Pete asked the room in general, but no one answered. They were not sure how Ned had come to his conclusion.

'No harm in letting the old boy try,' Tom Ladyburn said. 'If he has to change his mind . . .'

They went out into the night, stamping to keep their feet warm as they stood on the corner, and discussed the next morning's affair. Five men with guns. It should be plenty. Yet as Pete walked back to his home he felt uneasy. He hated having to kill a dog, no matter how savage. It always seemed wrong.

Far away from him, high on the fells, Nan hunted with the killer-dog, and her pup lay alone in the hollow tree. He had fed on a baby rabbit, and was not hungry. He could not understand why his mother had deserted him, nor why, when he went up to her, she turned her head and snapped, no longer interested in him. He lay and stared at the grass shivering in the wind that threaded minute crystals on every stem and twig and iced the dead flower heads with sugar-frosting, and curled himself tightly to try and keep warm.

CHAPTER SIX

THE men turned out at the edge of dawn, their spirits as bleak as the day that revealed brittle-frosted grass and heather hidden in grey-white blurring dust. The sheep were huddled for warmth. Small puffs of breath rose over each woolly head.

In the end, there were only four of them, as none of the others could spare the time from the day's chores. There were cows to milk and hens to clean out and feed, and pigs to see to, and those who did not work on the farms had jobs which started early. And nobody wanted a hand in killing a dog.

Tom Ladyburn carried the dead sheep slung over his shoulder. His face was grim. It angered him to lose a single beast, no matter the reason. He might only be hired man at Wellans', but he was a good shepherd, and Ted had a way of endearing himself to his men so that they never grudged him a second of their time and took a personal interest in his stock. Both Tom and Rob Hinney, the cowman, had been with Ted for years.

Ted himself was exhausted, after waiting up for his daughter, who came in after two o'clock, rebellious and unrepentant. The scene he had with her had kept him awake for the greater part of the night, his mind and stomach both churning, and not until just before dawn did he sleep, to waken thick-headed and stupid, knowing that he must go out with his gun and try and help catch the killer. There was more certainty with several men than with one.

Pete Lanark met them as he came down the hill from his own farm, having already looked over his sheep. Bet followed at heel, her face eager, loving every second of her

47

work. Now and then she pushed her cold nose into Pete's hand, assuring him of her constancy, and, asking for her reward, the petting which he never stinted. He nodded a brusque greeting, and waited beside the two men from Wellans.

The Huntsman toiled over the frosty tussocks, avoiding boggy patches that he knew as well as the foxes knew them, familiar with every inch of the ground, which he quartered year after year, seeking out new fox trails, noting where the quarry lay, taking heed of every scrap of cover, of every cranny and bolt-hole, and every place where the fox might maze his scent and check the hounds.

He was the smallest of the four men, yet no one was ever aware of the fact. He took his place among them, instantly alert to their moods. He noted Ted's haggard face as he would note an unusual feature on a fox track, and guessed its cause. He knew young Sue had been out with Jim Betwick again the night before. He had seen Jim's car parked at the end of Lover's Lane when he took his hound for its late-night walk, a walk that was a ritual for both Ranger and his master.

There was no need for words among them, and no desire for conversation. None of them cared to talk for the sake of talking. Pete and Tom, both used to long hours alone on the fells, with only the sheep and the dogs and the sky and the long slope to the far horizon for company, had few words, and disliked folk with the gift of the gab. Pete, in particular, often found his wife's desperate chatter most trying, and wished that she and the children would hold their peace.

Ted, sighting his rifle, looked up towards the distant peak, across ridged mounds covered with whitened grass, among which lay an occasional boulder, oddly like a crouching sheep. Beyond him, to the right, covering the angle of the field, was a thick clump of dwarf trees, their roots hidden by hawthorn bushes, the last leaves clinging forlornly to the branches. It offered a hiding place, and it was useless for the others, as they all had shotguns, and would be out of range.

He clumped off, glad to be on his own, aware of unspoken

sympathy, partly grateful, yet not wanting it, or, perhaps, wishing that he was not in a position to need it. A simple, straightforward man, who had always felt himself in full control of his family, he was bewildered and unhappy, and the knowledge that he was helpless and could not influence his daughter nor make her understand her parents' viewpoint made him surly and unsociable, so that everyone with whom he came in contact suffered from his tongue.

The bushes hid him completely, and he made himself as comfortable as possible; the rifle ready to use, the sights adjusted so that he covered the corner where the others stood, spying out the land.

Tom Ladyburn took himself to the far side of the hedge, where a gap in the branches enabled him to look upwards. He guessed that the dog would lie high at night, and probably shelter in a shepherd's hut, or one of the ruined cottages beyond the long wall that ranged for miles over the fell, marking the boundaries of Wellans' territory.

The sheep carcase lay where he had dropped it, beyond the hedge, on the open moor, and he could just make out the top of Pete's cap, as the other man knelt in the ditch, Bet lying obediently beside him, puzzled by her master's peculiar behaviour, but obedient, as always, to his instructions.

'Good lass,' he whispered now, and her tail twitched to show him she had heard. Her small sharp-muzzled head was lifted. Her eyes could see through the masking stiffened reedy grass to the giant boulder behind which the Huntsman hid, his shoulder just visible, mystifying her even more.

The Huntsman, looking over the fells, also saw a track marked plainly on the frosty grass. A fox had run here the night before, he guessed, scarcely disturbing the sheep as it passed. There were white feathers, just a few, caught by a twining snaky bramble shoot. Reynard had probably had duck for supper.

It was cold, with only the thin ghost of the early sun to warm them, and over each man's head plumes of smoky breath rose in tell-tale streamers. Pete pulled his coat collar close around his throat. Ted, the sharp twigs of hawthorn pressing against his unshaven cheek, flexed his fingers, hoping that they would not be too numb to pull the trigger. The Huntsman narrowed his eyes, watching for movement, any movement, no matter how slight, that might betray a racing dog, running to his last night's kill. Tom looking through the branch-patched gap in the hedge, his shoulders stooped so that he could see, blew on his hands and wished the damn dog would come and they could get it over with.

The sun rose red and streamers of scarlet fled across the sky. Ridged black clouds grew behind Horton Pike. A late owl jabbered its twittering cry. A hare fled up the hill, and Bet's ears pricked as she saw a flash of movement. A moment later, she caught its scent as the fitful wind backed. She did not move. Only her sniffing nose betrayed her interest.

Below them the village came to life. Smoke billowed from the half-hidden chimneys. Rob Hinney brought the lowing cows to the milking shed at Wellans, his cheerful whistle sounding thinly in the ears of the watchers on the fells. Pete, shifting awkwardly to ease a leg that had gone to sleep, wished that he were in the warm parlour among the steamy cows, and not here on the bleak hill, waiting to bring death to a living creature. Damn the dog. Why couldn't people train them properly? It wasn't the beast's fault that it had turned bad.

Discipline a dog, teach it, and see that it obeyed a command and didn't stray. And if folk couldn't, they shouldn't be allowed to keep an animal. Pete's thoughts ranged, trying to blot out physical discomfort. His feet were ice blocks, his fingers numb, and not even his heavy duffle coat could keep out the clawing wind.

Bad as lambing, when you walked among the ewes, watching, guarding against foxes, come for the cleansings, seeking those in trouble; always vigilant, while the wind whined through your clothing, and frost caught at your feet, and foxes lurked in the darkness.

Must be nice to be rich and build a lambing parlour, if that was what they called it. Pete brooded, thinking how he would like to have a huge building, like the one he'd seen written about in the FARMER AND STOCKBREEDER. A giant place where all the sheep were penned, and the shepherd had a room above them, a room with a glass wall so that he could look down on his charges and at once spot trouble.

A heated room with a bed to drop on for a few minutes, and warm water to wash in and a proper scrub up instead of relying on anti-biotic cream smothered on ice cold and often dirty hands. A place to heat milk, and fill bottles for the orphans. A warm place for the lambs, instead of bringing them home to lie in the outhouse, and struggling to rear them.

There was a movement on the hill. Bet lifted her head, and her ears pointed. She turned to look at her master, as if to confirm that he too had seen. He spoke to her softly, under his breath, and she relaxed, content.

The stray sheepdog was coming full-pelt, the bitch beside him, leaping at him playfully as she ran. Nan had forgotten the pup. She was enjoying herself, free of responsibility, keeping up effortlessly with the killer as he loped towards the scene of yesterday's crime.

The body of the ewe lay outside the field. The dog ran to it, tearing at the already mutilated throat. Three guns thundered. The dog rolled over, kicked, and was dead.

Nan, terrified by the noise and the strange behaviour of her companion, turned to flee over the heather, away from the sudden threat of danger. She leaped high over a clump of furze that barred her frenzied rush, and Pete fired.

The bitch tumbled headlong, over and over. The shot had been kind and her rapidly glazing eyes stared up at a sky that smouldered sulphur-yellow, dark with unshed snow, and hostile as the world into which she had been born. She died as she had lived, without a kind voice in her ears, or a friendly hand to stroke her.

The men, walking away from the scene of their victory, did not meet each other's eyes. Each one thought of his own dog and walked solitary beside his shamed shadow, head bowed, shoulders humped, rejecting the malaise of an unkind world that bred animals and neglected them, turning them into criminals.

On the hillside the pup waited, whimpering, lonely for the bitch who would never again warm him with her comforting presence, and never again put out an affectionate tongue to lick his upturned face.

CHAPTER SEVEN

LATER that day Ned Foley found the bodies of the two
dogs. Filled with pity, he stroked Nan's matted dirty fur,
and dug a grave in which he buried both animals together,
putting her beside the killer whose company had proved her
death warrant.

The sun had chased the frost away. The fells were warm
with brightness. Ned's small seamed face relaxed its grim
lines as he climbed towards the hollow tree. There was meat
in the parcel that he carried, and he wanted to make friends
with the pup.

The tree was empty. Ned looked about him, but there was
no sign of the little animal. He whistled hopefully, although
knowing that that would not bring a response. He did not
know where to look. Yet find the pup he must, or it too might
be condemned, and he was certain that, if tamed and trained,
it had a great future.

Nothing stirred except the grazing sheep. Far away, he
heard Pete whistle to Bet and saw Tom Ladyburn roving
among the Wellans flock, examining fleece and feet, his collie
singling each ewe from the flock to bring her to his master.

Ned pushed back his old cap and scratched his grey head
thoughtfully. He turned and plodded downhill, picking up his
spade as he passed the grave he had made. As he approached
his small house his dog heard his footsteps and barked an
eager greeting, thudding against the front door in a frantic
attempt to reach his master. A moment later Ned heard the
fox patter down the hall and yelp happily.

As Ned opened the door both animals hurled themselves
upon him, jumping up, licking his face, the fox as demon-
strative as the dog, having learned the dog's ways. It was

several minutes before the old man could quiet the pair of them. He took them into the kitchen, gave the fox a biscuit from the battered tin on the tiled mantel-shelf, and then hastily departed, flicking his fingers to the dog, which could not leave the house fast enough.

Ned watched as he ran ahead, a cross-bred, part lurcher, part collie, named Fleck. He ranged ahead of the old man, eagerly inspecting landmarks, sniffing ecstatically at clumps of grass, tail forever waving in delirious excitement at each new discovery, bounding up the hill, and then waiting, tail still weaving from side to side, head looking over one shoulder, until Ned caught up.

Ned led the dog to the tree.

'Find,' he said.

It was a forlorn hope. The bitch's scent must lie there strongly. Fleck did not hesitate. Nose down, he followed the trail unerringly, up the hill, across a wall, jumping it, and slithering into an unexpectedly deep ditch, skirting the edge of the field, over the wall on the other side, and on to the open fell, where the ruined cottage lay empty under the sky, its one remaining window filthy, blank and blind.

'Sit,' Ned ordered. The dog sat. 'Wait.'

Reluctant eyes followed him. Ned forgot his own dog. The pup was lying on the dusty floor of the old cottage, his eyes open, gazing at the sky. He saw the old man approach and, wary, bared his teeth in a long angry growl.

Ned stood still. Slowly, carefully, he lowered himself to the ground. The pup went on growling.

'Good feller,' the old man said. 'Fine feller. I won't hurt you. No one will hurt you. Why don't you give up and come and find a nice home, a nice warm place where you'll be safe, and fed!'

The growls had stopped. The pup was listening, his ears pricked, but he showed no sign of moving towards the man. It would take time, maybe more time than was available, though the pup was not nearly old enough to be a threat to sheep. Except that he might chase them, wanting to herd them, near to lambing time, and that would soon see the guns after him.

Ned went on talking, knowing that a soothing voice was always reassuring, remembering how he had talked all night to a bull caught in mud, to stop it struggling while the firemen worked to drag it out. Remembering how the stable man coaxed a road-shy horse, talking, talking, gentling, never raising his voice above a murmur. Remembering how he had tamed his first falcon, by babbling away, bits of remembered rhymes, sayings and thoughts and folklore, until the bird grew so used to the sound of him that he could approach it and lay a finger on its back between its wings and stroke gently.

It took time, so much time. He went on talking to the pup, while behind him his own dog watched. If the pup would approach the dog . . . if Fleck would be friendly, but that was not certain. His dog might be jealous. Didn't mind the fox, or the cat, but they had all grown up together, and now Fleck was nearly three, and might not accept a new member into his pack. Funny to remember that a dog was a pack animal and in a family he was either one of the pack with his master as boss dog, or he himself became boss and ruled the family. And that was a terrible thing, Ned thought, recalling spoilt dogs he had known, and the nuisance they were.

At last Ned stood up again. The pup backed, getting protection from the overhanging roof. He ignored it, turned on his heel, whistled to Fleck, and went off with as much speed as he could manage, down the hill again, leaving the paper wrapped parcel behind.

The pup watched him go. He could smell the meat, and he was starving. He had spent most of the night hunting on his mother's scent, trying to find her. At dawn he had discovered her dead body, and nosed it. Her lack of response and coldness terrified him and at last he ran to the cottage, too exhausted to seek the more familiar tree, which had also been an uneasy place to hide since the fox had killed his sister.

Hunger overcame fear. The pup approached the parcel cautiously. There was no sign of movement anywhere. He tore at the paper, chops slavering. Ned had brought a hunk of ox liver. The pup did not wait until the paper was torn

55

away. Paws on the parcel, holding it down, he began to tug at the meat, and gulped meat and paper together, until at last he was full.

That evening Ned returned to the cottage. The ruins were deserted, but he guessed that the pup would probably lie there, under the jagged roof, where the floor was dry. This time he unwrapped the meat, which came from a tin of dog-food. The pup found it when he returned from an unre-warded hunt, and wolfed it down.

By the end of that week the pup no longer hunted his food. He would not allow Ned near him, but he did not run away, and he waited patiently, listening to the noises that the man made, sounds that attracted him, though he did not know why and did not trust the talker. When Ned went, the pup fed greedily, and soon came to expect the visits, and to look anxiously at the man and make sure that he had in fact brought meat with him.

Also, the little dog was desperately lonely. He needed company, as all dogs needed it, and there was nowhere that he could find it. The man's visits helped assuage his misery. He was becoming dependent on them, even though any move-ment towards him brought an angry growl, and the savage snap of teeth.

Ned was paitent, and he had all the time in the world. His pension was enough for his few needs, and he could always earn a little on the side by beating for the city people who leased the shooting at the edge of the moor, or helping out with some of the many chores on the farms. Everybody knew and liked Ned, old rogue though he was, with his poaching ways, but he was honest too, according to his own ideas. The beasts, he felt, belonged to no one, and he was as entitled to a trout from the pool as the next man, but he would never lay a finger on another man's property, bought fair and square with his own hard earnings.

It was bitterly cold on the hill. Often the pup woke shiver-ing and ran in crazy circles to warm himself, sometimes chas-ing gaily after a shadow, or pouncing on a moving piece of grass. Then listlessness intervened. He needed the compan-ionship of man or of another dog, or to have a place of his own where he could lie up, warm and snug, a home place.

It was four weeks before he came to Ned's feet, and took food from his hand. Even then Ned did not touch him. He sat quietly, watching the small animal, that now, on a decent diet, was growing into a well-built dog. Dai Evans, the Vet, interested in Ned's efforts, had given him a vitamin preparation to add to the food, and make up for any deficiency the pup might have had. He might well have rickets, living wild like that. It was a common complaint in fox cubs.

Two nights before Christmas Ned changed his tactics. He brought food but did not leave it. He held it in his hand, a newly killed rabbit, the body still warm. At Dai's suggestion, he had left only a small meal the night before, and a token in the morning. The pup was starving.

He nuzzled the rabbit, but Ned was walking away and the rabbit went too. The pup followed, saliva running from the corners of his mouth, his eyes imploring, but the man ignored him, walking slowly and purposefully towards the village, talking softly and encouragingly, swinging the rabbit to and fro so that blood from it dropped at the pup's feet, making him frantic.

They paused at the edge of the fells, where the bridle path swung off into the village street. Ned dropped the rabbit. The pup seized it, and began to feed. Ned gave a deep sigh. He had been terrified that the little beast would grab the body and bolt for the moors.

The pup was so hungry that he did not see the man remove his jacket. Nor did he notice the jacket drop suddenly. Only when it covered him completely did he begin to struggle, and even in his struggles he held on to his supper, growling fiercely, kicking and twisting.

Ned held him firm. Tonight both dog and fox were shut in the outhouse, and the cat was out on his own business. It was not easy to hold the squirming body. The dog was more than half-grown and lean and muscular. But Ned had plans of his own. It was a bitterly cold night, and the pup had been shivering when he came for the rabbit.

At last they were inside, in the warm kitchen where firelight glimmered cosily on the walls. Ned switched on the light, and released the small animal, who stared about

57

the room, quivering with fright. Everything was strange. The little beast was overwhelmed with unfamiliar smells, traces from cat and fox and dog, the now familiar scent of Ned himself, the aftermath of food, and odd cloying unidentifiable odours from household items like soap and polish. In time he would become used to them and dismiss them, sorting out those that were important, but now they all spoke of danger, and danger of a kind that he did not understand.

Ned had put him on the mat by the fire, an old rough mat that had been chewed by countless animals, and that kept the background scent of otter and of hedgehog and of a young squirrel that the old man had fostered until it died, having been too small to be away from its mother. It had fallen out of its drey and been found by one of the village children.

The warmth from the fire was pleasant, although it was strange. It was soothing, reminding him, although he did not realize it, of puppy comfort when he curled against his brothers and sister in the cosy sanctuary provided by the hollow tree. He did not like the bright room.

There was an arm-chair behind him, a big wing chair, battered and worn by years of use. It stood on high legs, and beneath it, offering a dark refuge, was a cave, backed by the kitchen wall. The pup crept underneath, and took the rabbit with him. Ned settled himself in his favourite leather chair, pushing the stuffing back into the torn edge, and sat with his feet on the kerb, his empty pipe in his mouth, and an aura of satisfaction about him. Part of the struggle was over.

There were several problems to settle. The outhouse was cold, and it was not fair to leave his own animals outside all night. Fleck might tolerate the pup, but would the pup take to Fleck, and further, what would a pup bred in the wild make of the fox? He could not possibly bring them together. Not yet.

On the other hand, although the outhouse would be warmer for the pup than his ruined cottage on the high moors, Ned wanted him to settle for the night in a place where people belonged, to try and accustom him to men.

When he went to Pete he would sleep with the other dogs in the outhouse that was warmed by the Aga inside the kitchen, as the Aga backed on to the outside wall, but he would have to accept people handling him and also the children, and Johnny fussed every dog he met. The pup must be used to handling before Pete took him.

The gnawing sounds from under the chair ceased. Ned peered beneath, and saw the pup, exhausted by his experience, lying flat out and sound asleep, nose on paws.

Ned glanced at the clock. It was late and he was tired, and he still did not know what to do. At last he covered the kitchen floor deep in newspaper, piled coke on the all-night fire, fastened the guard firmly in place, and then shut the door. The pup did not move.

That night Fleck and the fox slept in Ned's own bedroom. Fleck curled by his master's feet, but the fox prowled the room and looked out of the window, gazing up the moonbright fells as if hungry for freedom, yet, every time that Ned let him go, he returned forlornly, unable to find a place for himself in the wild.

Just before dawn Blackie came lightly through the top of the window, surprised to find the fox and the dog in his own particular place. His astonished mew woke Ned, who guessed the cause, and patted the covers, but Blackie, determined to have pride of place, had his own ideas, and moreover, it had been a very cold night, as frost lay thick on the ground.

His ice-cold paw touched Ned's face as the cat pulled at the sheet determinedly. Ned opened both eyes and looked at the beast, which was a darker shadow among those that crowded the dawn-dim room. Blackie gave a quick throaty purr, and pulled at the sheet again.

This time a warm tunnel appeared, dark and inviting, and the cat was down it like a flash, curling himself up against Ned, right inside the bed, the air vibrant with his throaty satisfied purr. His cold paws dug against Ned's thick pyjamas, his cold moist nose rested against Ned's chin, and the old man grinned to himself, and stroked the thick fur, before he himself fell asleep once more.

The fox, inspired by this example, curled himself into the

hollow made by the old man's bent knees, and soon there was no sound in the room but the soft even breathing of the living creatures as they slept, and the busy tinny clicking of the urgent clock.

CHAPTER EIGHT

By morning, the pup had raged through the kitchen, and chewed, torn newspaper littered the floor. The tattered rug had been teased and worried, and Ned's slipper would never be the same again. Nor would the corner of the kitchen chair leg.

Ned sighed. He ought to have thought. Not as if it was the first pup he'd ever had. No use scolding him. The little beast would never know why he had been punished, so long after his crime. He lay asleep in the middle of the mess, but as soon as Ned opened the door, he fled under the chair, and crouched in the dark, watching.

Ned ignored him. He began to clean the kitchen, rolling up the paper and putting it on to the fire, talking to himself as he worked, moving slowly, careful not to make any sudden noise.

'You're going to be a handful, feller,' he said, sharply, aware of the cocked ears and the bright eyes that peered at him from under the chair. 'Dunno quite what we're going to do with you. Ought to turn you over to Pete to get you used to him, or you'll maybe not like changing masters. And you need a bath. Crawling with fleas and filthy. If I bath you now, you'll be scared of me for ever. I dunno what to do with you, that I don't. And a fine old mess you've made.'

It was done at last, and time for food. The pup smelt the dog meat as soon as the tin was open, and crawled out, his head protruding from the front of the chair.

'That's got you, has it?'

Ned put the meat on a saucer, put the saucer on the floor, and sat on a hard kitchen chair close by. He picked up the evening paper, and began to read. It had been left on the dresser the night before. The pup eyed him, and eyed the meat.

Minutes passed before he crawled out of his refuge, and came cautiously across the floor. Ned knew that if he moved the little beast would bolt for shelter again. He did not stir a muscle.

The pup began to eat, wolfing meat in huge gulps. In seconds the plate was clean. He sat and licked his chops, his busy tongue finding every last trace of food.

Ned picked the animal up from the floor, finding himself holding a tempestuous demon that bit, drawing blood. He stroked the fur between the pup's ears.

'Going to take time, isn't it, feller?' he said, putting the little beast down again. He washed the bite and cleaned it. It wasn't the first bite he had received, and it wouldn't be the last. He put on some ointment that the doctor had given him for such incidents, and then took food to the other animals, now in the outhouse again. Seemed a bit hard on them, he thought, as they begged to be let out.

He went back to the kitchen to make his own meal.

He was just finishing when Dai drove up in his Land-Rover, and hammered on the back door. The noise terrified the pup.

'Heard you'd caught the puppy,' Dai said, coming into the kitchen, banging his hands together. There was thick frost outside, and the air was barely warmed by the glowering red ball of the sun, low in the sky.

Ned gave a gap-toothed grin.

'They even know when you change your underwear in these parts,' he commented.

Dai sat in the leather chair and stretched his legs towards the blazing fire.

'Just come down from Wellans's. One of the dogs picked up some poison. Not heard of anyone laying it, have you, Ned? Looked like strychnine.'

'Could be Tanner,' Ned said, frowning. 'He does some damn' silly things. And he were saying Hunt don't kill off enough foxes, and he's had one after his chickens. Told him if he'd build a decent place for the fowls, he'd not have bother. But he's lazy as an adder in the midday sun, is old Tanner. Dog dead?'

'No. He'll be all right. Ted managed to get salt and water down him as soon as he guessed what was wrong, and I had some stuff that did the rest. Don't think it was a lethal dose, anyway, but I'd like to know who's laying the muck. There's no need for it, with these modern vermin killers. None of them hurt domestic beasts, and anyway, we've got a rat man, so no need for amateurs to try their hands.'

'Tanner's always been a lone hand. Remember how he tried to kill that badger on Josh Johnson's place? Smoked it out with sacking dipped in tar and petrol? Cor, that was a carry-on.' Ned, who had been busy with the coffee pot, poured out two mugs of thick black brew, topped them with milk, added heaped spoons full of sugar, and handed one of them to Dai.

'Needed that,' Dai said. 'Mrs. Wellans always gives me something to eat after a night like that but they were all upset and there was trouble with young Sue. Came in about two this morning and her Dad blazed at her. Not that I blame him. Young Mollie has to be home by ten or there's trouble, but maybe she's not got to the rebellious stage yet.'

'Mollie won't. She's not Sue's type.' Ned was positive, remembering how stubborn Sue had been as a child, and how different from Dai's eldest daughter, who laughed her way through most of her difficulties, and rarely took things to heart. Sue was the type who'd tie herself to the railings in aid of a cause, no matter how wrong she might be. And no turning her.

'She wouldn't fall for Jim, either, if I know Mollie,' Dai added. 'It's a shame. Changing the whole family, with Ted surly and his wife irritable, and even Rob was ratty this morning, and hadn't the time of day for me.'

Ned added more wood to the fire. He liked his neighbours, and felt sorry for Ted Wellans, who had often befriended him. He had his own opinion of Jim Betwick but that he was keeping to himself. He saw trouble coming, though what kind he was not sure. Sue might be flighty and silly but farmers' girls knew the facts of life and it wouldn't be that sort of trouble, or he didn't think so. Things were building up, and trouble at Wellans' could upset quite a few families, with Tom Ladyburn and Rob Hinney both getting bothered by Ted's manner, and upsetting their own families in their turn. No use asking for an odd job at Wellans', not unless he was invited there.

'So you got the pup.'

Ned sighed.

'Aye. I got him, and a right handful he's going to be. He's a fine pup, mind, but he's taken four weeks coaxing to get him here. And now he's here, I'm not sure what to do about him. He's too wild for Pete and it's not fair to my own beasts to have him here. Don't want him outside or he'll never get used to folk.' Ned filled his pipe, stabbing the tobacco viciously into the bowl, with blunt stubby fingers.

'Tom Ladyburn saw you drop your coat over him. Take time for him to forgive you for that,' Dai said. 'You've outraged him.'

'Didn't want to do it,' Ned puffed clouds of rank smoke. 'But I was afraid he'd freeze or be snow-trapped out there on the fells.'

'I doubt it,' Dai answered. 'Had a beagle brought to me last year. He'd gone missing in October and lived out through all that snow, and they found him again in March. He was as fit as if he'd been kept in all that time, in fact, a sight fitter, as he'd obviously had plenty of exercise. He'd been keeping himself too. One of the shepherds up there had often seen him with a rabbit or a hare, and he wouldn't go to any of them. His owner found him, almost by accident, taking the same walk as that on which he'd first lost him. The dog was sitting waiting for him as if he'd never been away.'

The pup was curious. His bright eyes peered out at them from under the chair. Dai ignored him, keeping only the corner of his eye on him.

'Think he'll tame?' Ned asked.

'Depends what you mean by tame,' Dai said, after a moment's thought. 'I very much doubt if he'll ever be as affectionate as a home-reared pup. He may not let anyone lay a hand on him. He's young enough, yet, though, and he's got sheepdog instincts. If anyone has patience and wants to

64

take the trouble ...' He shrugged. 'It's quite a challenge. You don't want him yourself?'

'Seems a shame to keep him.' Ned, too, was watching the movement beneath the chair. Although the pup was silent, his ears were cocked, moving as if he understood every word. Dai was aware that the small body was completely tense. The pup was far from accepting his new home.

'He'll miss his freedom.' The Vet drank the last of his coffee, and nodded agreement when Ned held up the pot. He passed his mug for a refill.

'He's a working dog. Once he's trained to the sheep he'll have all the freedom he needs.' Ned foraged in the cupboard and brought out a tin of biscuits. When the Vet had helped himself the old man threw one so that it landed just in front of the chair. The pup sniffed it, but it was not meat, and he crept back into his hiding place, leaving it untouched.

'Don't keep him too warm,' Dai said, yawning. 'He might go off his food if you do. He'd be better outside.'

'I know that,' Ned was suddenly irritable. 'How does he get used to being with people then? I'm not sitting all day in a freezing outhouse.'

'He won't be kept indoors when Pete gets him,' Dai added. 'It'll sort itself, things always do. Don't worry. And thanks for the coffee.' He yawned again, and went into the biting air. The pup bolted for the open door.

Dai fielded him, and was rewarded by a rumbling growl, and a snap at his gloved hand. He pushed the pup inside and slammed the door.

'I dunno what I'm going to do with him,' Ned said morosely, following the Welshman to the Land Rover. 'Easier with a wild animal. You don't want it dog-tame.'

'Or expect so much from it,' Dai said, as his big Labrador, on guard in the Land Rover, greeted him with a sweeping tail and an excited happy bark. 'Get over, Jet. I need room, too.'

The dog moved into the passenger seat and lay with its fore paws dangling towards the floor, watching as Dai put the vehicle into gear.

'Have you shown the pup to Pete yet?' he called out, shouting above the engine noise.

Ned shook his head. He could hear the desperate scratching at the door, as the dog whimpered to get out, begging for freedom. Blackie, who had jumped out of the window, walked delicately along the garden wall, and, reaching the back door, stared at it, turning questioning eyes on her master. She liked dogs, and would accept the newcomer, but what on earth would the pup do about the cat? Ned, standing on the frozen ground, scarcely aware of the cold that seeped through his old slippers, was reluctant to go indoors again.

Fleck and the fox whined to him from the outhouse. The pup whimpered again. Ned was overwhelmed by a sense of defeat. It would be kinder to let the pup go, to give it, for one more day, the freedom of the fells. It would return to the ruined cottage, and there, that night, Ned could take it meat. And swift release with his old gun.

The thought alone was treachery. Yet what else was he to do? He couldn't keep the pup, and Pete would be crazy to accept him. The little beast would never make a pet, and never make a working dog. Better a swift death when he was not expecting it than the merciless hunt that would track him down if the men knew he had been released.

Faintly, came the sound of bells, pealing over the fells from the little church. Puzzled, Ned listened, as the sounds increased, and a swift joyous lilt came into the ringing. And then he remembered. It was Christmas Eve, and they were practising the Christmas peal, as they always did.

Christmas. Silly, but he couldn't possibly shoot the pup at Christmas. Somehow, he felt better, now the decision was made. He'd give it till after the New Year.

And perhaps by then . . .

Whistling, he went indoors. The pup growled at him, and retreated under the chair. He went to find Fleck's outgrown puppy collar. Time for teaching to begin. Somehow, the pup had to learn, at least, to tolerate him, and also had to learn who was boss.

At the end of ten minutes the pup was wearing the collar. He was also wearing a determined expression, and sitting firmly on the floor scratching at the offending thing, determined to drag it off. Ned, his mouth set, dressed yet another bite, and restrained an impulse to take his chewed slipper and thrash the pup into submission.

He knew, that if he stayed, he would lose his temper, and that surprised him, for he was usually patient with animals. There was something about the pup . . .

He walked down to the *Swan* to have a word with the Huntsman. Perhaps he would have some advice to offer. But the Huntsman was ruffled, after words with Ted, who had stormed in to ask if Mr. Betwick was expected.

'Shoot the little beast and don't be so damned obstinate,' the Huntsman said sourly. 'He's too old to learn.'

'He'll be plaguing the lives out of the lot of us.' Tom Ladyburn had left his crook behind the night before, and come to collect it. It was his best dog that had been poisoned, and he was black bad-tempered, furious at the casual thoughtlessness that baited meat with strychnine and left it where a dog could get at it.

'I'd like to shoot the idiot that poisoned my dog,' he said, and added, 'and if the pup comes among my sheep, I'll shoot him, too, so look out, Ned.'

He slammed out of the door.

'Season of peace and goodwill,' Mrs. Jones said, shaking up a cushion as if she would like to kill that. 'What's got into everybody?'

Nobody answered her. Ned stamped off down the village street, wishing he had never set eyes on the dratted animal. He knew now that there was only one possible answer. But there was an easier way than using his gun. That night he would take the pup to Dai and have him put down. He could leave the little beast there and go away before Dai did the job. He could hand on the treachery and absolve himself from it.

The bells pealed merrily, mocking him as he went reluctantly to his house to see what further mischief the puppy had wrought while he was gone. He was tired and getting old and life held too many problems. And he had no Christmas dinner. He had forgotten all about that. Usually one of the villagers, or Mrs. Jones, sent him food or invited him for a meal. This year, they all had their own affairs to worry about.

Maybe, when he took the pup to Dai, Sheila Evans would remember him.

The church clock struck twelve. Midday. In another six hours it would be surgery time. He walked in at the back gate, and went to the shed to find a sack in which he could carry the little beast on his last journey. He felt like a hanging judge forced to confirm a death sentence.

CHAPTER NINE

THE pup spent the day beneath the chair, and Ned removed the collar, feeling that the dog might as well be free from irritation for his last few hours. He had intended to fasten a leash to it so that he could start teaching him cleanliness, but there was no longer any point. He dared not let the collie out. He would bolt to freedom.

By tea time, the old man was conscious of the hasty ticking clock, and the swift passing minutes. He fed the animals, giving the pup the best of everything that he had, uneasiness making him clumsy. Once he thought that the little beast suspected something strange. He was oddly subdued, cowering to the ground when Ned approached, which he had not done before. Perhaps he was sickening for some illness, or too hot in the warm room. It did not matter.

Ned was busy pouring boiling water into his tea pot when he heard a rattle at the back door. At first he thought it was the wind, but the sound came again, and when he opened it, he found Johnny, Pete's youngest child, standing outside, a bag held tightly in both small hands.

'Dad sent me,' Johnny said. 'Can I see your fox?'

Ned and Johnny were firm friends, and the old man's spirits lightened.

'He's outside,' he said. 'But come on in and you can see him in a minute.'

'These are for you. And Dad says Mrs. Jones forgot to tell you she wants to see you tomorrow, to have you to dinner. Mum's got a simply 'normous turkey,' he went on, the words spilling in haste. 'Only it's not dead yet, and I like it. I don't want to eat it. It's my friend.'

Ned grinned. There was always trouble at Pete's at Christmas. Johnny invariably became attached to the Christmas dinner, and the turkey always stayed alive while somebody hastily bought a dead bird from another farm. There would now be four unkillable and bad-tempered turkeys at Five Ways.

'Her name's Ellen,' Johnny added. 'And she likes eating grain out of my hand.' He skipped around the room, interested as always, in everything he saw, and then his memory made him dive into the bag. 'I made that for you, at school,' he added proudly, having just completed his first term. He pulled a badly wrapped parcel from the depths, and opened it himself. 'See?'

It was a calendar, made from coloured paper cut in the shape of a chicken, and stuck on to thick card. The calendar itself was crooked, and smudged with crayon, but Ned removed the old one from the kitchen wall and hung Johnny's in its place.

'That does brighten the place up,' he said admiringly.

'It's not very like a chicken,' Johnny said, looking at it thoughtfully. 'Its legs didn't go right. And paper won't look like feathers. You do like it?' he asked anxiously.

'I like it fine,' Ned was positive. 'You got time for tea, and then I'll take you home? It'll soon be dark.'

And it would delay the departure to the Vet, he thought, half hoping that Pete might ask him in and he could spend the time there until the *Swan* opened and he could delay his decision.

'They're all busy at home,' Johnny was glum. 'And Mum's cross. Too much to do, she says, and I'm underfoot all the time, and she made me put away my trains. I'm having a new engine, a green one, and, do you know something? I'm having a new puppy, did you know that? A puppy that can come right into the house and sleep on my bed, like Tony Martin's puppy does, and never have to sleep outside in the cold.'

This, Ned knew, was a pipe dream. Moira Lanark hated dogs and would never allow one in the house. She would not even go and look at Bet's puppies, saying the smell of them made her heave.

The pup had crept to the chair edge and was surveying the newcomer.

'There's my puppy. You've got my puppy,' Johnny shouted. The pup shot under the chair. Johnny flung himself on the floor and grabbed him by the scruff of his neck and pulled him out before Ned had time to say a word.

To his astonishment the pup did not resist. He lay, staring at the child. Johnny, a sturdy boy whose thin face had high cheekbones, a chinline that any beauty queen might have envied, and long lashed oval brown eyes, gazed now at the puppy with utter adoration, loving him so intensely that Ned could feel the child's emotion. He dared not move.

'I'm going to call you Rex,' Johnny said. He was an odd child, old-fashioned for his age, as he spent most of his time with his brothers and sister on the farm. Tony was fifteen and Ian seventeen and Rosalind almost nineteen. No one treated him like a baby and he was expected to help when necessary and behave himself properly. Without another child to set a bad example, Johnny was self-contained and rarely gave way to tantrums. As everyone ignored him completely when he did, there was little point.

'Rosie says Rex means a king, and I always wanted a dog called Rex. Only you won't tell Dad I've seen him, will you? He'll still be a surprise tomorrow morning when you bring him. I specially told everyone I wanted a puppy of my own, and I knew Dad would give me one. Perhaps that's why he sent me to see you. Can I take him home?'

Johnny had rolled on to his back and the pup was stretched out on top of him. Ned, astounded, found himself wondering if the pup recognized the child as being young and puppy-like, like himself, and accepted him completely. Or was it Johnny's fearlessness, or had the boy a way of his own with animals?

'See, he knows me, and he likes me. He knows he's mine.'

Johnny stood up, and lifted the puppy with him. The small tense body relaxed, resting in the child's arms, staring into the boy's face, bright brown eyes inscrutable.

Ned drew a deep breath, as he put a cloth on the table. He rarely bothered but he knew that Johnny loved a fuss, getting little attention at home, and being treated as an honoured guest was a novelty, to be savoured. The bag contained a roast chicken, and home made scones and little iced cakes.

71

Ned knew now that the child had been sent, with his own tea, to get him out of the way for an hour or two while the rest of the family prepared a surprise for him. Probably while they put up the Christmas tree. Ian, Johnny's eldest brother, had brought the boy to Ned the previous year, and again on the child's birthday. Now he could come alone.

'Mum said I could stay to tea if you weren't busy. The chicken's for your supper tomorrow. It isn't one of ours.'

Johnny climbed into the big leather chair, and sat with his legs crossed and the puppy lying in the hollow between his knees, small head on the boy's brown thigh.

'Can I take Rex home?'

'Not tonight, Johnny.' Ned felt harassed, not knowing what to do.

'Dad will teach him to guard the sheep, like Bet does. And then I can go out at lambing, in the night like Roy and Ian and take Rex and help the lambs be born. I like lambs. I like giving lambs their bottle. They suck and suck and pull and tug and make funny noises, like this ...' Johnny blew out his cheeks and made a guzzling sound, like a man noisily drinking soup. The pup sat up, ears cocked, head on one side, an intrigued expression on its face.

'Rex likes funny noises, too,' Johnny said. He laughed, looking up at Ned, completely absorbed and unself-conscious and happy. Ned was his friend, patient and familiar, helping his father at lambing time, always interested and philosophical about a cut knee, or stinging nettle blisters, and, when the boy was very small, he was more sympathetic than the family when, as Johnny frequently did, he fell in the midden.

Ned emptied the bag, finding chocolate biscuits and two Christmas crackers tucked away at the last. He put these on the table, while Johnny clicked his tongue, and blew raspberries and hissed and whistled and the pup sat on the chair, his head cocking, first to one side, and then to the other, his eyes brilliant with interest, his ears pricked, listening.

'He thinks I'm funny,' Johnny said ecstatically, his own eyes as bright as the dog's. 'He's laughing at me. Bet laughs too, she opens her mouth and puts out her tongue ...'

Johnny stuck out his own tongue and the pup reached up and licked it. Johnny shrieked with laughter.

'Your Mum wouldn't like that ... and I hope you're not catching his fleas,' Ned said. 'He needs a bath. He's a filthy little object.'

'I like fleas. Is tea ready? I like ticks too. Bet catches them off the sheep and Dad holds a lighted cigarette over them, or puts paraffin on and they go all shrivelly and fall off. If you pull them off they leave their heads in and make abscesses, so Ian belts me if I pull them. They're all fat and white and gooey ...' Johnny put the pup down on the chair and walked over to the table. His hands were so dirty that even Ned noticed.

'Soap and water first, young man,' he said, pointing to the sink.

The pup watched the boy walk across the room. He remained on the chair but, as a knock sounded on the back door, he jumped down and bolted for his own private sanctuary. The door opened, and Jasper Ayepenny put his head inside.

'Come on in, Jasper,' Ned said, and then remembered Nell, but it was too late. The red setter was already inside the room, sniffing curiously. She went over to the chair under which the pup had taken refuge.

'She can smell my puppy,' Johnny said. He grinned up at Jasper. 'I've got a puppy for Christmas. He's all my own puppy. His name's Rex, and I told everyone I wanted a puppy for Christmas and now I've got one. Isn't that good?'

Jasper glanced sharply at Ned, who shrugged helplessly.

'Johnny came in and found the pup,' he said.

'That pup's a mite wild,' Jasper said cautiously, knowing its history and knowing the trouble Ned had had with it.

'I like wild puppies,' Johnny asserted. 'You come to tea, too, Jasper, and we can have a party. Mum made enough cakes. She's cross because she doesn't like Christmas and she sent me down to see Ned.' Johnny bit deep into icing, enjoying his tea all the more because Ned had not bothered with bread and butter, and then, quite suddenly, he put the cake back on the plate and stared up at the two men with terrified eyes.

73

'They've sent me here so's they could kill Ellen,' he said frantically. 'That's why they sent me, so's they could kill her. I don't want to eat Ellen. She's my friend.'

'They sent you here because they were busy. They won't kill Ellen. They never have killed your turkey yet, now have they, Johnny?' Ned asked, and then catching sight of Nell, added, 'Look at the dogs.'

Johnny turned his head. Nell was lying on the hearthrug, her head bent as she licked at the pup, which was snuggled close against her, as if to derive from her warm body all the comfort that had been lost to him. His tail moved in gentle pleasure, and he lifted his head and licked Nell's nose.

'Funny,' Jasper observed. 'She's like that with all young things, yet never a litter of her own. Reckon yon pup's just bewildered, Ned. He'll like enough come round in time. He lets the boy play with him?'

'He loves me,' Johnny said firmly, his mouth full of pink iced cake. 'We've got a Christmas tree bigger than the house,' he added, swinging off at a tangent. 'As big as big, and Dad had to cut the top off. Have you got a Christmas tree, Jasper?'

'Bess 'as got a little one, and she's baked a big batch of gingerbread men for them as comes a-carolling,' Jasper said. 'Shouldn't wonder if there was one to spare if you came calling in the next day or two, and a little something hidden on the tree, too.'

'Bess makes lovely gingerbread men,' Johnny said dreamily, sucking the chocolate off the end of a chocolate biscuit and inspecting the end to see if he was down to plain biscuit yet. 'They have currant eyes and a cherry nose and a lemon peel mouth and currant buttons and great big clowny feet. I like Bess. I like everybody,' he added expansively, and then frowned, 'Except Ian, when he belts me.'

'I expect you deserve it,' Ned said, pouring another cup of tea all round. Johnny inspected his cup gravely, appreciating the rich brown brew, so unlike the milky tea his mother gave him. He added four teaspoons full of sugar, as a further assertion of independence and grown-upness.

'I wrote my name in his book. I wrote JOHNNY in big letters all over the writing and Ian belted me and Mum was cross. Please can I have that chocolate biscuit?' he added, grabbing it hurriedly before anyone could say no.

'Not surprised he belted you,' Jasper said. 'Nobody writes in books.'

Johnny contemplated this statement and seemed to find it lacking in logic.

'I did,' he said definitely and nodded his head twice, firmly. 'And Mum belted Ian for belting me. Only when Ian said why, Mum wouldn't give me any sweets after dinner for a whole week. It wasn't fair. It was a silly old book, anyway, all about cows' illnesses.'

'What's wrong with that, then?' Ned asked, wondering just how a child's mind did work.

'It ought to be about sheep's illnesses. We've only got three cows. Cows are silly things. Except yours, Jasper,' Johnny added generously.

The quick rat-tat on the back door made them all jump, and the pup left Nell and fled under his chair again. The setter turned her head to look at him, astonished by his behaviour.

Ned called out, and Pete Lanark opened the door.

'Reckon you've had enough of that limb of mine,' he was beginning, when Johnny hurled himself from his chair and grabbed his father's legs tightly, burrowing his head against the thick solid thigh.

'I love my puppy. Can I take him home with me? Thank you, thank you, thank you,' he said, all on one breath.

Pete raised his eyebrows and looked at Ned.

'That the pup you were talking about?'

Ned nodded.

'Not my doing . . .' he said unhappily, not knowing what to do about the situation.

'He's here, only he's shy and a bit dirty, only we can bath him and then I can teach him and he'll be the best sheepdog ever and I can help with the lambs like Roy and Ian . . .'

'Hey, hey, hold on a minute,' Pete protested. 'Let's all get our breath back, shall we? Where's the pup?'

'Here,' Johnny said, and went over to the chair. Pete followed, and crouched down and peered underneath, seeing

75

nothing but a bright and wary pair of eyes regarding him with a decidedly hostile expression. He advanced one hand. The pup growled.

Johnny pushed past his father, reached for the pup, pulled him out, and taking him by the skin on both sides of his neck, shook him soundly. 'Bad, bad, bad!' he said angrily, over and over again.

Ned held his breath, too terrified to intervene, while Pete, unaware of the pup's savage ways, watched with mild astonishment.

'That's how a sheepdog gets punished if he's bad,' Johnny scolded. 'You're not to growl at people. It's naughty. Bad dog.'

The pup was too astounded to growl again. Johnny had shown his mastery in a way that he could understand, for that was how Rex dealt with his own enemies, by shaking them thoroughly. He needed reassurance, and he crawled to Nell, legs crouched, tail down, giving the men a wide berth.

'See? He's good now,' Johnny said. He flopped to the hearthrug. His sleek dark head, with a persistent fringe that fell over his forehead no matter how his mother combed it, leaned confidingly against Nell's flank. He rubbed his other hand gently over the pup's back, sleeking the fur, murmuring, while Ned wondered if he should tell Pete that he had decided to have the pup put down. Certainly it seemed quiet enough now. Perhaps he had handled it wrongly . . . he just didn't know.

'One thing's for sure . . . we can't take him home looking like that. Your mother would have a fit,' Pete said, eyeing the pup closely. He was in a filthy state. Burrs tangled his muddy matted coat, and one eye needed attention, oozing from a tiny scratch in the corner. Moira, who disliked all dogs, would insist he was destroyed.

Ned looked at the pup hopelessly. He had thought perhaps Johnny would provide him with a way out. He doubted if, even now, the pup would take to him. He reached with his hand. The pup growled viciously. Johnny shook him again.

'Johnny,' his father said. 'He'll bite you . . .'

'No, he won't,' Johnny said with supreme conviction, and

put his small face down to the pup, who licked his nose. 'See?' He grinned triumphantly at the men, pleased to be, for once, a centre of attention.

'Tell you what,' Jasper said diffidently. 'It's school holidays. Suppose the pup stays here and Johnny comes every day and helps Ned teach it? Then by time term begins, you could take him home and carry on from there?'

'Sounds a good idea to me,' Ned said, relief showing so plainly that Pete wondered just what had been going on. 'What's more, if Jasper and Nell come too ... the pup likes Nell, and Jasper's taught so many pups, he can tell us what to do, eh Johnny?'

'Keep him out of his mother's road, too,' Pete said. Moira found the youngster very trying, after so long without small children in the house, and Pete privately thought she was far too hard on him. Kids needed a bit of fun. No use telling Moira, though. She was a good woman, a religious woman, and she did her duty, but she hated the farm and country ways. She'd been so gay and bright and fun-loving herself when he'd married her, and now the years had turned her sour. Funny what time did to people.

'Can I come? Every day? And have dinner and tea with you, black tea like we had today? And will you poach a trout? Mum says you're a reprob ... – a something ...'

'Johnny!' Pete said warningly, and added hastily, to distract attention, 'You can only come if you're good. And now you've made me forget what I really came for. Moira asked you up for this evening ... the carol singers are ending at our place, and she's put something on the tree for you both.'

It was a long-standing custom, started from the days when the older children were small. All those who helped on the farm during the year were welcomed in for a drink and sandwiches and mince pies. Pete enjoyed every second of it, but for the past few years, since Johnny was born, he had been aware that Moira was more and more reluctant to carry on the old custom. The kid tired her, he supposed. Tonight he'd persuaded Rosie to help her mother, but she was newly engaged and tied up with her boy friend, not wanting to spend any time at home.

Ned was covering the floor with newspaper.

'You'll have to learn to be clean,' Johnny said, and shook his finger at the pup. The boy rolled over, and discovered a tag end of rope lying on the floor near him. He held it over the pup's nose, and the little beast grabbed it, growling and worrying and shaking his head, in a glorious joyous tussle such as he had once had with his brothers and sister up on the fells.

Johnny, his face flushed, his eyes laughing, tugged at the other end, and Nell watched them, stately with age, and tolerant, loving both puppies and children with equal fervour.

'Time to go home, Johnny. You can come again tomorrow,' Pete said.

Johnny put his arms round the pup.

'I'll be back,' he promised. 'You be good.'

The pup watched them go. Ned, glancing down before he switched off the light, saw with satisfaction that the little beast had not crawled under the chair, but was lying where they had left him, looking longingly at Nell.

'Stars!' Johnny said with satisfaction, looking up at the sky as they went out into the village street. 'That one's the Christmas star.'

He pointed to a particularly brilliant shimmer above the church spire, and as he pointed, the first carol singers started on their rounds.

Clear and sweet on the frosty air came the sound of the lilting voices.

'We sing that at school,' Johnny said.

And all the way up the hill, walking beside them, his hand in his father's, his small tuneless voice sang the words to them.

> 'I had no gifts to bring . . .
> Prr um pum pum pum . . .
> . . . . . .
> And He smiled at me,
> Prr um pum pum pum
> Me and my drum . . .'

Oddly, as he walked towards the lighted farm under the

glitter of night, Ned felt that there was a hidden inner meaning to the words, one that he guessed at, and almost knew, but could not fathom. And then, as the final words died away, he caught the elusive meaning and knew that Johnny, without anything except his own will and determination had brought a gift for the pup and reprieved his death sentence.

Their heels rang sharp on the cobbled yard, and as they came to the farmhouse door all four of them broke into sudden carolling.

'Give ye heed to what we say . . .
Joy, joy, joy . . .'

As background to their singing came the exultant peal of the Christmas bells.

CHAPTER TEN

NED never forgot that Christmas holiday as long as he lived. It seemed, even in retrospect, to be a frantic muddle of child and dogs, a never peaceful racketing that went on and on, and ended so suddenly that he felt completely bereft, when Johnny took the pup home and school began.

He woke on Christmas morning to the sound of frantic knocking. Startled, he switched on the light and peered sleepily at the clock, which had apparently stopped. He shook it, and shook it again. It was only half past five.

Something must be wrong. Jasper was ill, or one of the other neighbours, or a cow had fallen in a ditch, or a horse was endangered. The fox sat up and stared, and Fleck watched sleepily from one half-open eye as Ned struggled into a reprehensible old tartan dressing-gown and shabby out-at-toe slippers, and hurried downstairs. The dog woke to reality and followed, barking at the closed kitchen door.

The noise at the back door was thunderous. Ned opened it. Light, streaming from the scullery, fell on Johnny, standing in a thin drizzle in the dark garden, his face rosy under the bright yellow sou'wester, his mackintosh buttoned wrongly, his Wellingtons on the wrong feet.

'Johnny!' Ned said, in astonishment.

'Can I see my puppy?'

Ned rubbed his bristly face, and then pushed his hands through his hair, so that it stood on end, spikily defiant.

'Does your dad know you're here?'

'Dad's milking early so's he can take Mum to early service, only I don't have to go. I said can I get up and Dad said yes, and I said can I come down and Dad said yes, and I watched him milking a little and then I said I'm going to see my puppy and then I runned.' Johnny screwed up his eyes as if he were trying hard to remember. 'I think he shouted only I didn't hear properly 'cos my boots made a noise on the ground.'

'You'd best come inside,' Ned said, yawning and smothering a laugh. 'There's no point in me catching my death.'

The pup was underneath the chair, his expression dubious, but when he caught sight of Johnny he wriggled out, his tail wagging his whole body. Ned looked at him in astonishment.

'He knows me!' Johnny shed his outdoor clothes hurriedly on to the floor, and knelt down and grabbed the puppy, which licked his face furiously, making small pleased whimpering noises.

'Well, I'll be darned,' Ned said to himself, busy with kettle and tea cups, and turning up the damper so that the all-night fire roared into a blaze. He flung a large log on to the flames, hating the smell of coke, which he only used at night to keep the fire in.

'Happy Christmas, Ned,' Johnny said, when he had his breath back. He felt in his raincoat pocket. 'I got a present for you today, too. It's a fishing hook. I found it on the river bank last year,' he added proudly.

Ned took the rusty hook gravely and thanked the child, and hunted on the dresser, where he had put a bright new half-crown the night before. He put it on the plate that he had set for Johnny.

Another knock thumped on the back door.

'All the world's calling at crack of day today,' Ned observed, dragging the door open. 'Come on in, Ian, and Happy Christmas.'

'Happy Christmas!' Ian said, disgust in his voice. 'Where's that young Johnny? I'll slay him, running off and waking you at this time. Johnny, come out of there.'

Ian was Johnny grown-up, his dark curly hair rebellious, the brown eyes surly, above them dark eyebrows that flared outwards and upwards in perpetual surprise. The hooded duffle coat added deceptive bulk to his tall slender body.

The pup was under the chair, peeping at them anxiously, and Johnny had hidden himself behind it. His face, when he peeped out at his brother, reflected the pup's anxiety.

Johnny was very much afraid of Ian, who was stricter than either of his parents.

'Let the boy be, it's Christmas,' Ned said. 'I don't mind, honest I don't. I'd got to get up, anyway. Things to do. Makes a change to have folk calling at this time,' he added. 'Not as if I was a slugabed. Often just coming home now.'

Johnny crept out hesitantly.

'Dad didn't say I couldn't come. I told him,' he said defensively.

'And never waited for an answer,' Ian said angrily. 'Johnny, you're the limit.'

'I never had a puppy before, not a puppy of my own,' Johnny said. He looked up at Ned anxiously. 'Are you cross, Ned?'

'Not at Christmas. But not so early tomorrow, young'un. Now let's clear up and have breakfast.' Ned bent to roll the soiled newspaper, and then picked up a bitten and chewed and sorry looking object and stared at it. 'Land's sake, that's my brush. Have to put a muzzle on the pup at night!'

'He's getting new teeth,' Johnny said. 'My pony's getting new teeth. She chews the edge of her stall, all night long, she chews and chews. I'm getting new teeth too,' he added proudly. 'Look, this one's all wobbly. I can wobble it with my tongue.' He opened his mouth to show them.

'You'd best be quiet lest I change my mind and lam you,' Ian said, grilling thick rashers of bacon while Ned laid the table, cut bread into doorstep hunks, brewed the tea, and fried eggs. Johnny sat stroking the pup's thick fur.

'I got a box of chocolates and a book to read and crayons and a humming top in my stocking,' he observed, looking into the fire. His mind shot off on a new tack. 'If you look hard at the fire there's a little tiny house with smoke coming out of the door, and it's all on fire. Our hay caught fire last year, and we had the fire engine, and I saw the hose. And the firemen. And the fire engine. And the—'

'Mind like a butterfly,' Ian said grumpily. 'Never concentrates for a second.'

'No more did you at his age,' Ned said, putting food down for the pup, and for his own animals. There was a sudden whining and scratching in the passage. Johnny grabbed the pup and held him tight, as the door, which had only been part latched, burst open, and Fleck and the fox came bounding in. They saw the pup and stopped stockstill.

The fox, after giving Ned a brief welcome, sat down and stared at the intruder. The pup growled warningly. The fox, interested, pricked his ears, and continued to stare, unwinking, his mouth open in a mildly amused gape.

Fleck, knowing Johnny, ran up to him with wagging tail, ignoring the pup. Johnny greeted the dog. The pup redoubled his threats. Fleck sniffed him, and then, suddenly contemptuous, went over to Ned and began to fuss him furiously, as if to demonstrate that the man belonged to him, and no outsiders were going to have a share.

'Put the pup down and see what happens, Johnny,' Ned said.

'They won't hurt him?' Johnny's face was anxious.

'Don't think so. Just try it and see.'

The pup crouched on the mat. He could not reach his chair without passing the fox, which continued to stare at him unnervingly. Fleck bent his head to sniff the newcomer, his tail wagging slowly from side to side, as if he was uncertain how to behave.

A moment later, he pounced at the pup, and pushed him over. He stood above him, looking down, tail wagging amiably, eyes bright, ears pricked. The pup rolled on to his back, and looked up at the dog standing huge above him. He lay there, front paws curled, submissive, finding the smell of another dog comforting. Fleck eyed him, and walked back to Ned.

'They'll be O.K. now,' Ned said. 'Pup's too young for them to hurt, and he's decided not to try anything on them.'

'Have to bath him,' Ian said sourly. 'Filthy little brute. He'll never make a sheepdog.'

'That's where you're wrong,' Ned pushed a plate of bacon and eggs across the table to Johnny.

'Two eggs!' Johnny said. 'Two eggs!' He began to eat hungrily, too busy with his food to listen to the argument that flared across the room.

'He can round up sheep as if he'd been trained,' Ned said. 'I've seen him.'

'Maybe round them, but there's more to it than that,' Ian said sourly. He was annoyed because he had had to get up early. It was not his turn. He and his father milked the three cows, that they kept for milk and cheese and butter and cream, on alternate days.

Ian found Johnny far more of a pest than did the other two, and, moreover, his temper was short because he had a mind for Sue Wellans and she only had eyes for Jim Betwick. Ian's opinion of Jim Betwick was unrepeatable, Jim with the huge allowance that his Dad made him, and his flashy, fast car and his dare-devil risk-neck tom-fool driving – he'd kill himself and Sue one of these days. There wasn't a girl to touch Sue ... his thoughts went round like a millwheel, round and round on the same track, never deviating, and his temper worsened daily. He took a lot of it out on Johnny, who suffered for Sue Wellans' sins.

'Dog's got to learn obedience. This one'll never learn. Got a mind of his own.'

'He'll learn,' Ned repeated obstinately.

Johnny finished his breakfast, tearing his bread into pieces and using his fingers to drag it through the egg that remained on the plate.

'Johnny, you're revolting,' Ian said angrily.

Johnny looked up at his brother, pondering a cheeky reply, caught his expression and, instead, sighed deeply, and climbed off his chair.

'Come on, Rex,' he called, enticing the puppy, who was lying thoughtfully under the chair again while Fleck and the fox commanded the rug by the fire.

The pup could not resist Johnny. He crawled out, and the child laughed at him, reached out a hand, rolled him over, and rough-housed his fur. The pup, delighted, snapped and snarled and bit, but this time it was mock fury, puppy fun, the kind of game that he had played with his litter brothers.

Another knock sounded on the door. Ned grinned.

'All the world and his wife coming calling today,' he said.

Pete stood on the doorstep, his face grim.

'Want a word with young Johnny,' he said. 'And Ian. Sent him to fetch the little blighter back, not to stay and eat with you.' His eyes roved over the breakfast time debris.

'My fault,' Ned said. 'It's Christmas time. And not often I got company. I was making the most of it.'

Pete looked at him.

'Ned, you'd charm the heart out of a stone mannikin,' he said at last. 'You better come up and have a drink with us to celebrate Christmas before going off to eat yourself stupid at the *Swan*.'

Ned laughed.

'I'd better smarten meself up first,' he said. 'Mrs. Jones won't save any turkey for me if I go wi'out a shave, and your good lady won't like it, neither. You go along with Ian, and I'll bring young Johnny.'

Pete sighed. Moira was angry, and their Christmas had a blight on it before it had ever begun. Johnny had not even stopped to share his stocking with his mother, as he had always done before. He was growing up too fast, and she resented it. Not that she encouraged him to be a baby, but she liked to think he needed her still. The others no longer did.

Ian was always brooding, Lord knew why, and Rosie with her mind full of moon and stars, and white weddings, and all because of young Colin, nice enough lad, but not one you'd think would set bells ringing the way they seemed to Rosie's head. The lass lived in a dream. Never heard a word said to her. And Tony, full of ideas and too big for his boots and needing his ears clipped more often than not, and a sore trial to everyone.

'I'll wait here,' Pete decided. Moira would bridle her tongue if Ned was there. If it was just family . . . he shrugged and sat wearily in the big chair.

'I'll get off,' Ian said sullenly, knowing that if he went the long way round past Wellans', he might catch a glimpse of Sue and wish her a Merry Christmas, though goodness knew it wouldn't be merry for him. She scarcely seemed to know he existed, let alone toss him a smile or a look. And if he did see her, all dressed up and probably off with Jim Betwick, he'd only be mad. Life wasn't worth living. He went out and slammed the door. The pup jumped.

'Dunno what's up with Ian,' Pete said morosely, watching Johnny roll over and over with the pup in his arms. He'd clean clothes on for Christmas and they were already grubby. His mother would grumble even more, but too late now. The damage was done. The pup certainly needed a bath badly.

Ned, busy shaving at the sink, his knees bent so that he could see into the low, cracked, and brown-mottled mirror, grunted. His cut-throat razor needed all his concentration. At last he was done, and he wiped the lather off his face.

'Happen he's in love. Right age for it,' Ned said.

'Why didn't you get married, Ned?' Johnny asked, his face buried in the pup's fur, his voice indistinct but the question clear enough.

'Dunno.' Ned thought, frowning. 'There was a girl, once, but she wouldn't have me, and I didn't want no one else. Women chatter and cry and make you wipe yer boots and get uncommon cranky.'

'Mum gets uncommon cranky.' Johnny wiped his sleeve across his face, smearing both skin and sleeve.

'That's enough, Johnny,' his father said sharply.

Johnny looked at Ned from under lowered eyelids. Ned met the child's gaze with a stony face, ranging himself on the side of the adults, anxious not to encourage naughtiness. Johnny lowered his eyes. The long lashes swept the brown cheek. The pup licked the shut lids, and a moment later Johnny was laughing, chasing the pup under the table and behind the chair and into the scullery and back again, while Fleck looked on tolerantly from the sanctuary of the basket chair, and the fox, after one startled glance, jumped up and sat on the table, in case he was trodden on during the romp.

Ned banked the fire, and shut dog and fox into the scullery, not wanting to trust them with the pup in his absence. Johnny dragged on his mackintosh and scrambled into his boots.

'I want to take the puppy home,' he said, looking up at his father with blandishment in his brown eyes.

'When he's clean and bathed and trained a bit,' Pete said. 'Your Mum would never bide him now.'

'It's not fair,' Johnny began, but this time it was Ned who intervened firmly.

'Life's never fair, young Johnny, not to no one, and don't

86

you ever forget it. Why should it be fair, then? You make the best of it. There's folk that's happier in little huts than ever in big palaces. And you have to learn to wait,' he added. 'Nothing's worth having that's come easy.'

Johnny only understood half of what Ned was saying, but he quietened down and walked sedately between the two men, his high spirits leading him now and again to an excited little hop.

Everything was fascinating in Johnny's world. As he walked along the frosty lane, he saw with eyes that were clear and fresh, and found each sight new and wildly stimulating. There was a spider's web in the hedge, a perfect wheel, and the frost had rimmed it and the sun shone on it and fragile droplets of glistening glory hung in beads along every flimsy line. He stopped to stare, putting out a small finger to try and catch a rainbow trapping dewdrop, and then caught up with a skip and a jump, gripping Ned's hand, only to let it go again when he saw a blackbird sitting on a high twig on a rowan-tree, tugging at a few last berries, the sun sheening his feathers to brightness.

The bare hedge, revealing the sites of old nests, was suddenly tangled with twisting masses of Old Man's Beard; mystifyingly hoarding things that other people had thrown away; part of an old wheel, a rusting, broken pram, and then, in the road, lay Johnny's own personal miracle, a shining new nut, fallen from some farm vehicle. There might be a bolt at home to fit it, or he could tie it to a string and swing it round his head and then let it go to fly satisfyingly far, or perhaps, even though it was not round, it would roll.

He tucked it into his pocket, where he already had two conkers and a twisting tangle of string, a battered swan's feather, the quill broken and the vane tattered and dirty, a midget tractor that went everywhere that Johnny went, even to school or to bed, and sat on the edge of the vast bath at bedtime, waiting for him to finish. He valued his treasures with all the greed of a miser. The metal nut was something to stare at and gloat over, and see how it was made, the inside part a little rough to small fingers, the outside burnished and shiny and with scratches on it.

Bet and Sam were waiting in the yard. They hurtled to

welcome Pete, jumping up at him, tails weaving, bodies twisting. Sam, as always, uttered short exultant barks, but Bet made an odd groaning noise, a most peculiar sound that was reserved entirely for her master, and with which she greeted no one else, though Pete had heard her use it once when she returned to one of her litters after a particularly long absence.

'Down!' he said as he came to the farmhouse door, and both dogs dropped immediately, their eyes saddened, their whole attitude drooping. The wagging tails were still. They hated being left outside, but knew the house was forbidden. Now there was nothing to do but wait until Pete came back to them and excitement could begin again, with a long walk on the fells, checking over the sheep, a chore that could not be neglected, even on Christmas day.

The house was so warm that it made the men gasp, newly come as they were from the fine clear frosty air. Johnny stared around him, loving the Christmas kitchen, loving the baubled tree, the streamers and tinsel stars that hung from the rafters, the smell of cooking food, the hot mince pies, the vast table, partly laid for dinner, an immense iced Christmas cake in the centre, piled bright wrapped crackers around it, the unusual sight of wine glasses, and the best china, and the little Christmas trees and snowmen that came out year after year to decorate each place.

He breathed in the scent of pine needles, stared at the coloured lights that Pete had just switched on and the unguessable, mysterious shapes of the brown paper parcels on the floor round the tree, at the holly sprays with the scarlet berries and the mistletoe, its own berries pearly clear. He never tired of looking at the Christmas house, so much more beautiful than everyday.

Moira came bustling out of the pantry. Her fair hair was greying, her features blurring, and she had put on weight over the years. She was a tall woman, and would have been better looking if discontent had not brooded on her face. She put down the vegetables that she was carrying, saw Johnny and gasped.

'You dirty little Arab!' she said. She would have said more, but Ned came forward with a beam on his face and a vast sheaf of chrysanthemums he had wheedled from Jo Needler at the nursery, and wished her the season's greetings.

The shimmering room, more like a magic cave in a fairy tale than a room in an everyday house, went to Johnny's head completely. He forgot that Moira was angry with him, forgot his dirty clothes, forgot that he had run from home at five in the morning, and rushed at his mother and grabbed her round the waist.

'I do love you! I do love Christmas. I do love my puppy!' He shouted into her apron, almost sick with excitement. Moira looked at the men helplessly.

'I've got a new puppy, did Dad tell you? His name's Rex. He's going to be the best sheepdog ever and win all the trials and be better than Sam and better than Bet and better than ... better than the bestest there ever was.' Johnny had to stop for breath.

'Another dog?' Moira's voice was bitter.

Johnny looked up at her, his expression changing to dismay.

'We need another dog,' Pete said. 'Bet's eight and getting on, and Sam's four. It's time for a youngster, or I'll be left without a sheepdog some day. I was going to get one anyway.'

Moira picked up the vegetables.

'Go and get washed and put on some clean clothes,' she said to Johnny.

Chastened, he crept away.

'A dog of his own will do him good,' Pete said. 'He doesn't get much fun. Like being an only child, with the others so much older than he is.'

'Life isn't much fun, and the sooner he learns, the less disappointed he'll be later.' Moira sliced brussels' sprouts viciously. She hated dogs and she hated sheep, hated the stinking smell of them that clung to her menfolk and never seemed to leave the house, hated the silly bleating baas that plagued her at all times, hated the mess and the constant sheep talk. Talk of the price of wool and shearing time, and liverfluke and sheep tick and maggots and foot rot. Talk of lambing and the lambing troubles and the new sheep dips, and every penny Pete made going to build a better flock, a stronger flock, as if there was nothing else in life but sheep.

And just when she thought she might get some freedom and a chance to get away sometimes and not be so tied, Johnny had come along. She loved Johnny, yet she resented him too. She pushed the hair out of her eyes with a wet hand. Behind her Ned and Pete were toasting Christmas. Ian had come into the kitchen, seen them and slammed out again. Rosie had gone for the day to her fiancé's house. If only she weren't so tired, Moira thought desolately. If only she'd had the sense to marry a man who built houses, or sold motor cars, who came home at nights to talk to her, instead of being out in the fields with those silly dogs. Pete might as well be a dog, she thought, bitterly. He understood dogs much better than he did her.

Johnny had crept back into the kitchen. He was clean again, and had put on the new jersey she had just finished making him, and his brown cord trousers. He looked enchanting. He gave her a wary look, and she immediately felt guilty. Poor kid, he hadn't much fun. Had to be grown up all the time, and see to himself.

'There's a mince pie for you to eat with your lemonade,' she said, and watched his face brighten. It took so little to make him happy. 'What are you going to call your dog?' she asked, as he poured out his own drink.

With that one sentence she opened the gate of heaven for Johnny. He looked up at her with brilliant eyes.

'Rex,' he said. 'Rosie says Rex is a king's name, and he's a king dog. He's beautiful,' Johnny added, adoration in his voice. Pete thought of the scruffy little beast on Ned's rug and grinned. Wonderful what a kid could see if he wanted to.

Johnny, chewing his mince pie, had his first wish of the season, and now he sat, the farm kitchen forgotten. He was out on the fells with his sheep. The biggest flock of sheep that anyone had ever seen. Their woolly backs were massed together for as far as his eye could reach, and round them, herding them, obedient to the tiniest flick of Johnny's finger, went the most handsome sheepdog in the whole world, his tail and back and head in one long beautiful line, his coat glistening, his wonderful eyes cowing the bold ewes that sometimes turned to defy him.

'Here, Rex,' Johnny said. 'Good lad,' and the dog came, and looked up at his master, and the two of them had no need for words.

'Wake up, Johnny,' Pete said, laughing. 'What are you dreaming about?'

'Nothing,' said Johnny, and took another mince pie.

CHAPTER ELEVEN

THE pup was intelligent and quick to learn, so long as he wanted to learn. He was responsive to a tone of voice, and although he never did allow Ned or any other adult to touch him, he knew at once whether the spoken word meant approval or disapproval.

Dai, coming to examine him, was forced to muzzle him before he could handle him.

'About five months old, at a guess,' the Vet said. He patted the angry little beast. 'We'd better bath him.'

It was easier said than done. In spite of the muzzle the pup resisted with every ounce of his strength. Soaped and slippery, he jumped out of the water, and Johnny, chasing him and calling him, tripped over the kitchen stool and banged his eye on the corner of the table. He stood, blinking slow tears away, conscious, temporarily, only of the pain.

A moment later, both men stared and Johnny looked down. The pup had come to him, as if aware of his hurt, and was gently butting against the boy's leg, licking at his free hand, tail wagging in sympathy.

'That was your fault, Rex,' Johnny grumbled. He blinked the tears away. 'Now come and be good.'

Dai tied the home-made muzzle again, and Johnny dumped the pup in the water, which splashed all over the floor. By the time they had finished they were all wet.

Ned made tea for Dai while Johnny took the holey old towel that was kept for the dogs and rubbed the pup dry. Before more than a few minutes had passed the drying had turned into a crazy game, and Rex teased and worried the end of the towel, pulling at it, until Johnny was helpless with laughter as the pair of them struggled together on the mat.

Long before the dog was dry they were both exhausted, and when Ned poured the tea and passed a cup to Johnny he found boy and dog curled up together, sound asleep.

'Wish I could fall asleep like that,' Dai commented. 'That's a handsome little beast, good lines to him. Pedigree somewhere, I should think. Wonder whose bitch that was?'

'Didn't belong to anyone round here,' Ned said. 'Wondered meself. If the pup makes a good sheepdog Pete'll want to enter him for the trials. And he can't stand for the International without a pedigree.'

'Don't think Pete would go for the International,' Dai said, yawning. He had had three broken nights in succession and was on his way to see a cow over at Wellans. She'd calved but the cleansing hadn't come away. Funny how some cows calved easy and others always had trouble.

'Bit far and a bit expensive,' Ned agreed, stirring his cup vigorously.

'Pup house-trained?' Dai asked.

'He's coming on fine. Very quick to learn. Only got to say "Bah" to him and down goes his tail and he slinks off to that old chair there,' Ned said, nodding.

Dai laughed.

'As he's doing now. He wasn't so fast asleep as you thought, and I bet he's wondering what the dickens he's done now, poor little beast!'

'It's O.K., lad,' Ned said hastily. 'Good dog.'

Bewildered, the pup wagged his tail half-heartedly, and then sat and looked at the men, as if unsure whether to continue to behave as if he had been bad, or to take notice of the reassurance.

'Darn it,' Ned said. 'Undo half the good I've done. Good lad. Here, then.' He threw a biscuit. The pup raised his head and snapped at it, catching it in mid air.

'Isn't he clever?' Johnny was awake, stretching and yawning, his gap-toothed mouth grinning widely. He patted the pup. 'He knows his name and nearly always comes when he's called, and he sits. Sometimes he sits,' Johnny added, anxious to be honest.

'Don't teach him too much too soon,' Dai said. 'He'll get bored, just as you get bored if people try to tell you too much. And if you ask him to do something, don't let him get away with not doing it. He must do as he's told, or he'll never be any use with the sheep.'

Johnny nodded, unaware that he was learning along with the pup.

He loved the long days with Ned, and with Jasper and Nell. Ned would take them to the fells, and show him where the fox had lain the night before, the holt where the otter had reared her cubs last spring, the weasel's tracks in the slimy mud on the hill path.

Together they watched the crows come back to roost, saw the hare leap up the mountain side while they held Rex tightly by the scruff of his neck and he shivered with excitement and longing, remembering wild chases over the moor when he had lived with his mother in the old hollow tree.

The pup wore a collar now, and Johnny held him on a long rope, as Ned was afraid that freedom would call him. Their walks were not always dignified. Rex hated the confining lead, and sat, refusing to budge, or stood with his paws firmly planted, pulling against the tug which urged him forward.

Before the Christmas holiday had ended he learned to walk where Johnny walked, and came more willingly. He inspected every bush and tree and heather clump, his tail waving, as familiar scents came to him ... the scent of the ranging fox, of rabbit or hare, or mole, the clean tangy scents of the bruised growth under their feet, the smell of dank leaves, the tantalizing urgent memory of a deer that had lain to sleep in a sheltered hollow.

The weather remained frosty, the ground metal-hard under their shoes, the grass crisp and brittle grey, as if dusted with sudden age. Feeding on the moors was sparse. The fox became bold and took a duck from Wellans', the badger left his tracks in the cowpats as he hunted rats near the stacks, and one day, as Ned took Johnny and the pup by a less frequented route, they saw an astonishing sight.

'Down,' Ned said and the dog crouched at their feet, and Johnny, under Ned's hard fingers, crouched too, and stared at the flock of birds gathered on the fell some yards in front of them, entirely unaware of their presence.

In the centre something span and weaved and twisted, snaky sinuous. The watching birds came nearer and nearer, the lithe body curved and tumbled, the pup, catching the scent, trembled and whimpered, and before Johnny could restrain him he ran, with a swift bound that tore away the rope from the boy's hands, towards the acrobat.

A cloud of birds flew into the sky, their beating wings making the pup jump backwards, but the enticing scent was more than he could bear, and he hurled himself headlong. The weasel, baulked of a meal, snapped viciously, catching the pup on the nose, and then turned, while he was still shaking his head, and slid along the path and vanished without a sound.

'Here, Rex,' Johnny called, and the pup came back miserably, blood dripping from a gash across his muzzle.

'Only seen that once before in my life,' Ned said. 'Wanted you to see it. I was going to throw a stone before old weasel pounced. He'd 've ended by suddenly jumping at a bird. Proper hypnotized, they are. It's queer.'

Johnny looked anxiously at the bite on the dog's muzzle.

'That won't hurt him. Heal in a day or two,' Ned assured him.

Jasper, who had been plodding slowly and painfully up the hill behind them, came up with Nell. The pup greeted her with a small pleased yelp, and she went to him and nosed him and, then, sympathetic, licked the cut across his face.

'Nell'll clean it for him,' Jasper said, watching the pair with amusement in his blue eyes. Nell stood over the pup, her once-slender body bulky with age, although there was spring in her step and she could chase after Rex until she tired of the game, and bowled him over to show that she had had enough.

Rex, beside her, was now a long-legged animal, his feet seeming too big for him, with all the clumsy gaucheness of adolescence. His tail knocked cups off the table, and he blundered over himself, always active, urgent and eager, longing for a romp with either Fleck or the fox or Nell, will-

95

ing to accept all of them, yet greeting any adult that approached him with a lifted lip and silent angry snarl.

'Don't trust any of us,' Jasper said, watching the collie as he ran friskily beside the setter, jumping up at her shoulder, and barking excitedly. 'He know his name yet, Johnny?'

'Rex!' Johnny called shrilly. The pup turned his head and stared, and Johnny flicked his fingers as he had seen his father flick to Bet. 'Here, boy. Good dog, then!'

Rex left Nell and came, at first reluctant, and then, remembering Johnny and apparently convinced that they had parted hours and not a few minutes ago, he hurled himself at the child, upsetting his balance so that Johnny went sprawling and landed, laughing, on the soft slippery grass, while his dog licked his face, leaving blood from the still seeping weasel gash on Johnny's coat.

'Your Mum'll have something to say about that,' Ned observed. 'Best get back and clean it quick before it's had time to settle.'

At tea that afternoon, Johnny gave a deep sigh, and stared forlornly into the cup of dark brew.

'Troubles of the world?' Jasper asked, a grin quirking his lips. It must be wonderful to be five and have a five-year-old's woes only on your shoulders, though maybe they were as bad to the boy as Jasper's aching legs and back and difficulties with his pension were to him.

'It's school tomorrow,' Johnny said, forlornly. 'I wish I never had to go to school. Just play with Rex all day and come down here with Foxy and Fleck and Nell.'

'Never make a farmer if you don't go to school,' Jasper said. 'Got to learn to figure out cost of sheep and rams and price you get for wool, and price for cattle feed and sheep feed and sheep dip and Vet bills ... got to know how to read so's you can tell where the next auction is and what beasts you want to put in and what you want to buy ... got to know how a tractor works, and cost of fuel for it ... got a mighty lot of learning about living to do yet, Johnny. Wish I'd had the chance to stay at school ...'

His mind went back suddenly over the long years to the day he was twelve and sent down the valley to a strange farmer to learn his job. He could recall every minute of that day, from breakfast with the men, after four hours of hard work, at nine o'clock in the old kitchen, where the black leaded grate shone bright and reflected the flames, and they ate great slabs of grilled ham with fried potatoes.

Through to milking and the cows pushing at him, no fancy machines then, but down on the stool with the bucket at your feet, and your head resting on the warm cow, and a soft tuneless whistle that kept the milk flowing. They hadn't let the milk down properly for him for weeks, he remembered, hating the feel of his unskilled hands pulling and botching, and that morning old Nowty, he'd forgotten her real name, she fetched him a kick that spilled the bucket and sent him sprawling in the muck and the men had laughed at him.

After that they'd been out in the frosty fields for the turnips, and then a spell of fence mending, with the icy wire cutting and tearing at hands that were still tender with youth. And out muck-spreading and hay-spreading for horses and cattle, and him no bigger than a half grown calf himself, and having to work like a man all the time, and all for four shillings a week. Kids now didn't know they were born.

'Time for milking,' he said, coming back to the present with a start of surprise as the ratty old clock chuntered the hour. 'Twitchett don't like being kept waiting. She'll open the gate and be out of the field and holding up traffic if I don't go and see to her.'

Ned grinned. Twitchett was a determined character and well known in the village, always leading her four half-sisters home if Jasper was more than ten minutes late, and come clock changing time there was trouble for weeks, and usually Jasper gave in and milked at the same time by Greenwich the whole year round, rather than have the policeman for ever at his door with news of complaints about unattended cows straying up the road.

Jasper eased himself slowly, using the edge of the table to pull himself out of the chair. Life was getting uncommon painful, he thought grimly, aware of a knifing ache in the back of his legs, giving him news of the night to come when he would lie wakeful, hearing the church clock strike each quarter, unable to find a position in bed that gave him ease or comfort.

'Night, young Johnny,' he said, as he waited for Nell to come to him. 'Make the most of it while you can.'

Make the most of what, Johnny wondered, looking to see if anything had been left from tea. But the table was bare. He huddled on the rug with the pup straddling his knees, and looked at the fire. Fleck and the fox, now reconciled to the collie, lay sprawled beside him, watchful, for sometimes the boy trod on them accidentally.

'Rex won't like sleeping in the outhouse,' Johnny said.

'He's got to get used to it, like you've got to get used to school.' Ned shouldered into his thick coat. 'Time for home, Johnny. Give the pup a chance to settle, and you a chance to get your things ready for school.'

'I don't want to go to school,' Johnny repeated stubbornly.

'Guess that's how the pup'll feel, too,' Ned said, as he slammed the house door shut behind him. Rex, hating his leash, followed Johnny miserably. Ned was afraid that the pup, allowed freedom in a strange place, would take to the fells again. 'Rex has got to start school too. You and your Dad will be teaching him how to look after the sheep. He's got a lot to learn, soon as he's old enough. No use having a sheepdog that won't take orders. And this time, you'll be teacher.'

Johnny grinned suddenly.

'I'm going to teach Rex,' he began to chant. 'I'll teach Rex! I'll teach Rex! I'll teach Rex!'

His voice grew louder and louder as they hurried up the hill to Five Ways, and by the time that they reached home Johnny had quite forgotten his reluctance and was eagerly looking forward to the end of the next day, when he and the pup would, for the first time, go out with the sheep.

'I'll be as big as Ian and as big as Tony and as big as Tom Ladyburn and as big as my Dad,' he said, as they turned into the yard. 'I'm going to have the biggest sheep farm in all the world and Rex will be the bestest dog.'

Ned laughed as he turned away. Johnny took his dog and put him in the outhouse.

'You'll have to be good,' he warned. 'You can't come in-doors, not here.'

The pup settled on the straw, and Johnny went indoors, but at bedtime he was missing, and Ian finally found him fast asleep in the chilly outhouse, with the collie cuddled tightly against the child's body.

CHAPTER TWELVE

LIFE, for Johnny, began each afternoon at tea time. School was something to be endured, although he worked as hard as any five-year-old was able, and managed a certain amount of fun. But time was only real when Rex was there.

Pete, who asked little of the pup while he was young, soon found that the collie had no use for anyone but Johnny. The bond between boy and dog grew stronger daily. Rex waited for Johnny's footstep, pricked up his ears and came wholeheartedly alive only at the sound of Johnny's voice, and though moderately obedient and reasonably submissive, no one could hold him when Johnny came home from school.

No matter where the dog was, he seemed to know the time, and promptly at four each day he was sitting by the gate, his attitude one of patient expectancy as he looked anxiously down the road. When at last Johnny came in sight he began to bark his welcome and by the time the boy reached the farm, Rex was berserk with happiness, racing in small circles until he could fling himself with full enthusiasm at his master, licking face and legs and hands, wagging his whole body with his violently waving tail, while Johnny hugged him, and then joined in a crazy romp that started with the dog bringing an old worn slipper which the child tried to drag from him, and ended in a delirious chase.

By the time winter had warmed into spring and spring given way to high summer, the dog had grown out of leggy puppyhood, and was becoming a handsome glossy black and white collie with a determined eye and a firm way and a mind of his own.

His real training had not yet begun. Pete, taking him to

the fields, found him so enthusiastic about herding the flock that he could not call the eager little animal from his task. Each time a sheep broke away the pup brought it back, determined to keep the herd packed, and each member of it under his domination. He did not need Pete to show him what to do, but he needed to learn discipline, to learn to stop when called, to deny the urgent imperative command that was inherent in his ancestry and that he could only obey and not understand. He had to herd.

Left free in the farmyard, he herded the hens, herded the ducks, and tried, just once, to herd the cats. He herded the bags of grain in the barn, the milk pails against the wall, the churns outside the dairy. He herded the three cows at milking time.

'Never seen a pup like him,' Pete said, half laughing, half exasperated, as he pulled the collie away from the ducks for the umpteenth time, and shut him in the outhouse so that the poor birds might be free to waddle down to the pond again, where, as far as Pete could make out, the pup seemed to think they were in danger of drowning so that it was his absolute duty to keep them away from water.

Between Pete and the pup there was some understanding, but Rex allowed no liberties. He did not growl at the farmer, but he did not encourage any form of caress, and only Johnny was ever greeted with real pleasure. For Pete there was an acknowledgement, a token wag of the tail, and a cautious watchfulness.

'I wish he'd be more forthcoming with me,' Pete said to Ian, as Bet and Sam came chasing back to him, jumping at his hand, and Rex, who had been taken out to the fells for the first time on his own without Johnny followed more sedately, and then, as if a clock had struck in his mind, realized suddenly that Johnny would be coming home from school any minute and fled for home, ignoring Pete's shouts to him.

'That dog's going to be a dead loss,' he said, suddenly furious. 'And it's no use punishing him for running to Johnny. Trouble is, he's more of a pet than a sheepdog, and that's all he ever will be.'

'He's a thief, too,' Ian said. He was still morose, taking

every chance he had to look out for Sue Wellans, who barely gave him a look and still spent more time than she had to spare with Jim, racing from place to place in the little scarlet sports car that was now a byword as it squealed round the corners of the country lanes, and sped, exceeding the speed limit, along the motorway, flashing off the miles while Sue exulted and Jim drove faster and faster to please her.

'A thief?' Pete signalled to Bet to bring him a ewe that was hobbling along with a length of wire tangled round one leg. Bet brought her and stood expectant, waiting for praise, wagging her tail frantically when Pete gave it. He removed the wire, slapped the old ewe on the rump and sent Sam to take her back to the herd again, just to give him practice, for the ewe knew her own way as well as the dog did.

'Ran into the kitchen yesterday and stole tomorrow's supper – a leg of lamb. Mum was gunning for him, but she never found him. He took it into the barn behind the bales. Found the bone this morning. He's a devil, that dog.'

Summer had almost ended when Johnny got measles, and lay, feverish and unhappy, too ill to eat or drink for several days. Moira, busy and bothered, shut the dog in the outhouse until his howling drove her mad, and then, when he was released, he lay under Johnny's window, his nose on his paws, showing no sign of happiness or pleasure at anything.

Bet tried to cheer him, as if aware of his loneliness, but he snapped at her, and, irritable with heat and edgy with temper, fought Sam until both dogs were bleeding, and Pete and Ian had a struggle to separate them. After that he was chained each day, and he grew more and more morose. At night he slept alone in the outhouse while the other two roamed free, and went for shelter to the barn if the night was wet.

By the time Johnny was recovering, and fretful with convalescence, the collie's temper was so unpredictable that Pete began to worry about him, wondering if he would become completely savage again before the child was well enough to get up and comfort the dog. Once he suggested that Rex was allowed in the house, but Moira would have none of it. She hated dogs at the best of times, and the collie was so snappy that she was afraid of him. He sensed her fear, and, not understanding it, barked whenever she came near him, adding to her woes.

The day that Johnny was to come downstairs for the first time Pete let the collie out of the outhouse. The dog stood at the gate, as if remembering his life on the fells, and suddenly cleared the wall with a bound, and, in spite of Pete's frequent calls, flung himself headlong down the hill towards the beck.

It was a brilliant day, a rare day, with the sun high in the sky, and wind enough to cool the blaze of noon. Wind that stirred his coat, reminding him of days long ago, of free days on the fells, when no man had commanded him, and no woman chased him. Johnny had gone, and was gone for ever, and Rex was free again, having no desire to attach himself to anyone else.

He stopped to savour the cool of the beck, the water rippling over his paws. He waded, and, finding a pool, he swam, savouring unusual pleasure in something that he had never attempted before. He shook himself, standing on the bank, the bright drops flying from him, and then, finding the lure of rabbit, loped through the brushy heather, eager for the well-remembered taint.

The rabbits were snug below ground. The dog stopped to sniff at a burrow. He dug, but half-heartedly, and then, remembering Johnny, lay with his paws stretched out and his nose resting on them, and sighed and thought, while Johnny, just got up, ran round the farmyard calling desperately, and then, when he could not find the dog, cried himself sick so that his temperature raced up and Moira sent for the doctor again and cursed the wretched brute that had caused so much trouble.

By mid-afternoon Rex was tired. There had been no sign of food for him and he had lost his skill at hunting. He was hot, and he loped slowly over the fell towards Tanner's place.

Tanner, farming with a minimum of trouble, had found himself rat ridden, and there on the ground behind the haystack, was half a rabbit, laid out as bait.

Rex fed well. Nobody saw him come or go, and Tanner

would not have cared if he had. He had little sympathy for man or beast, and the villagers reciprocated his feelings, having no time at all for him.

Full-fed, the dog turned for home. Perhaps Johnny would be there, after all, coming up the hill from school. The collie made a detour, and herded the sheep in Tom Ladyburn's field, moving them so gently that Tom did not even suspect a dog among them and thought that they were going of their own free will, away from some scent or sight bothering them by the hedge.

There was a meeting at the Church Hall and the car park was full. An errant impulse made Rex herd the cars and an amused councillor, looking through the church hall window, saw the collie crouching, cowing a big Ford with an eye that threatened doom to anything that disobeyed him, and then, with a firm movement, slink forward and snap at the wheel of a small three wheeler that was apparently defying him. The work amused the dog, and for a moment his tail beat happily, and then he remembered Johnny and went off anxiously, back to Five Ways.

By now Johnny was in bed again, sobbing in a desultory fashion that upset Rosie, who was sitting with him. She heard a small whimper and looked out of the window.

'Rex is home,' she said.

Johnny sat up, his eyes wide, his face dangerously flushed and streaked with tears.

'Show me!' He commanded.

Rosie wrapped him in his dressing gown and carried him to the window. He leaned out.

'Rex! Rex!' he shouted.

The dog lifted his head, stared in disbelief, and was transformed. He streaked through the farmyard, turned in at the kitchen door, pelted for the stairs, and arrived, demented with joy, in Johnny's bedroom, where he could not show his pleasure enough, and raced crazily round the room, jumping up, barking, licking the boy's hands, wagging his tail and then his hind quarters, until finally his whole body was a single undulating wave of pure ecstasy and Johnny, half laughing, half crying, was put back on his bed, to pat the dog with both hands and say over and over again, 'Rex! Rex! Rex!'

Moira Lanark, coming into the room with Johnny's tea, set her lips.

'Mum, let the dog stay, please,' Rosie begged. 'Look, Johnny's looking better already.'

Reluctantly Moira agreed, and soon Johnny was sound asleep, his flush reduced, his hand gripping the dog's fur tightly, so tight that when at about midnight the poison began to work and the dog cried out in pain, and then went into a convulsion, he woke the child, who screamed at the top of his voice.

Pete came running.

He took one look at the dog and swore viciously to himself.

'That bloody lunatic, Tanner,' he said, forgetting the child.

'What is it? What's the matter?' Johnny stared at the collie, terrified. 'Is he dying?'

It was no use comforting the boy now.

'I don't know, Johnny. I'm going straight to the Vet. We'll do our best.' If the dog will let us, he thought, as he bent to pick the collie up. The convulsion had stopped. The dog was sick, shivering violently, but he seemed to understand that Pete was trying to help and he did not struggle when the man lifted him.

Rosie, coming in at the door, her face startled, her dressing-gown pulled round her, her long hair in two pigtails, making her look twelve instead of nineteen, gave one look at the dog.

'Poison?'

Pete nodded.

Ian appeared, saw his father's face, and raced back to his room, to emerge again pulling trousers and a jersey over his pyjamas as he ran downstairs. Moira, exhausted after several nights of sitting up with Johnny, came into the child's bedroom just as the Land Rover roared off into the night.

'What on earth's wrong?' she asked.

'Rex has been poisoned,' Johnny said, and Rosie grabbed him tightly as the slow desolate tears spilled out of his eyes, and he stared into a bleak future, in which his wonderful dog had no place.

CHAPTER THIRTEEN

DAI EVANS was a dedicated man and an obstinate man.
Death was a personal enemy, each beast that he failed to
save both an insult to his skill, and a challenge, so that he
spent much time in taking note of treatments, in watching
how an animal responded to his care, until he seemed to have
an uncanny insight into the stages of a disease and the behaviour of the suffering animal.

Few people realized that his knowledge came from persistent observation, that every tiny reaction gave him a new
clue, and he kept notebooks which he filled up on his rare
free evenings with queries, with records, and with new
ideas about future treatment, varying dosage and drug until
men from miles away called on his skill, knowing that if any
man could save a beast, Dai Evans could.

His big untidy ramshackle house and neglected garden
were always overflowing with animals. A lame badger cub
played with a pair of abandoned fox cubs; a young deer, the
mother shot out of season by a thieving youth from a distant
town, skipped gaily in the paddock with three ponies, one
of them far too old to work, but living out his last days in
Sheila Evans' gentle care.

Nobody quite knew how many dogs there were, for
most of the strays ended here in an unofficial dogs' home,
and the Evans children advertised them at school, usually
finding a good home for a neglected pup. The strays came
from the town. No villager would take a dog and then
neglect it, except Tanner, who had twice been prosecuted
by the R.S.P.C.A. and now took a little more care, knowing
that another prosecution would stop him from keeping dogs
altogether and no farmer could manage without.

Apart from anything else the dogs guarded the place, and on several occasions men pretending to be travellers in cattle foods, or dealers in livestock had come to the villages, looked around, and returned later to steal what they could. Nell, Jasper's setter, had let one of them into Bess's back yard, where he, sure of privacy, had helped himself to the tools in the little shed. He was just carrying them out to his car when the setter gave the alarm, and penned him helpless, threatening him with her teeth whenever he moved.

Jasper, returning from taking the cows to pasture, found the pair of them, and, with a sly grin on his face, decided to walk to fetch the policeman, rather than phone, and leave the man stewing a while longer in Nell's competent care. Ben Timmins had never made such an easy arrest.

Dai knew all the beasts in the village, and all the men. He heard the Land Rover racing up the hill, its engine labouring, and before the vehicle turned into the yard behind his house where his clients parked their cars, he was out of bed and half dressed.

The bell screamed its summons.

Sheila woke drowsily, saw her husband dressed, and was about to settle to sleep again when some instinct made her change her mind and reach for slacks and a heavy jersey.

'No need for you to come, love,' Dai said, vanishing through the door, hoping to silence the bell before the children wakened. Their busy curiosity was not always welcome, and they shared his defeat if his patient died.

Dai took one look at Rex. The dog's body was arched, his back strained, his teeth showing through drawn back lips. He had no awareness of anything around him.

'All right. On the table with him, quick!'

Dai was already busy, syringe in hand, summing up the situation, wondering how much poison the dog had taken. Strychnine was tricky ... depended how much experience the poisoner had. Why couldn't they stick to the branded rat poisons that only killed rats and did no harm to domestic animals? Lord knew they were advertised in all the farming journals.

There was little time for talk. Little time for anything but the dog on the table.

'Johnny's beside himself,' Pete said.

Dai nodded.

He knew what it was like to have dogs in the family. His youngest child always formed violent attachments to those he was unable to keep. He could not bear to think of her when her own dog died . . . perhaps that would not be for a long time. Perhaps stoicism came with age.

'Come and have coffee, Pete,' Sheila said from the doorway. 'Best not to watch. Dai knows how it's going, and there's no need to give up hope yet?'

It was not quite a question but Dai interpreted it, and catching his wife's eye, he frowned warningly. The dog was very bad. No use giving hope unnecessarily.

Pete, sitting in the kitchen, the Aga opened to give extra warmth and the sight of a cheerful glow, held his coffee mug between his hands and brooded over it. Odd, now he was aware that he had a warm feeling for the dog and he had thought it a pest and a nuisance only a few hours ago. They had had the little beast for nigh on six months and it had made a lot of difference to Johnny. The child had the dog to play with, and each new day was bright with excitement, with the morning before school made bearable by the collie's boisterous welcome, and homecoming something to be eagerly looked forward to. Also, the dog kept the child out of Moira's way and out of mischief, so that she was more relaxed, and the family did not suffer so often from her bitter tongue.

Sheila did not interrupt him. None of the villagers were chatterboxes, and she herself was tired. She yawned. It was going to be a long night, and she doubted if Pete would leave. Ian had already gone, walking home to bed, so that he could be up early to milk the cows and then take Bet and Sam out to see over the sheep. The lambs were still half grown and skittish and almost every day saw one or more in trouble.

Only two days before he had had to climb down to a rocky ledge under a ramshackle wooden bridge to rescue one that had slid down the steep miry bank, and been trapped, unable to climb back. Lucky it had gone no farther. There was a forty foot drop over which water roared in a terrifying cascade to fall into a deep pool below, a pool which was always ice cold and shadowed from the sun on even the hottest day.

Ian was gone from Pete's thoughts almost as soon as the door closed behind him. He could only think of Johnny. His last born child was his pet, and, now he himself was older, the boy kept him young and entertained him. He liked having the child along when they looked over the sheep, liked teaching him, and also Johnny had a deep feeling for animals that the others lacked. The child seemed to know instinctively how an animal felt, whether it was facing him boldly, unafraid, or was terrified of him, and he could adapt his manner to win its trust.

Ian was like Moira. He knew he would inherit the sheep farm one day, and he did his share, but he had no love for the job. It was a job, and no more. And lately he had been far too difficult to live with. It was a relief to turn from Ian's surliness and frequent rudeness to Johnny's chatter and his wild pleasure in his father's company, and his feeling for his dog. Tony was still at school, and too busy playing in the teams to spend time at home. And Rosie was bemused by her approaching wedding, even though it was probably eight months off.

'Tanner's a devil,' he said morosely, preferring a new tack of thought.

'It would be Tanner,' Sheila agreed. 'Only trouble is that Rex was straying on Tanner's land, and there's no proving anything, anyway. Tanner won't have meant to kill dogs.'

'Wouldn't put it past him,' Pete said irritably. He brushed his hand over the dark thatch of hair that was so like Johnny's.

'Not him. One of his own dogs took poison a bit ago, didn't you know?'

Pete shook his head.

'The dog died. Tanner brought him here too late. Poor beast was half starved too. Probably hadn't any strength to resist the stuff.' Sheila poured more coffee, and fetched a plate of scones from the pantry and buttered two of them. 'Tanner still doesn't learn,' she added, spreading butter thick.

'Always do get hungry when I get up at night,' she said, laughing at herself. 'And I need to slim. Plump as a Christmas goose, I'm getting.'

'You don't need to stay up,' Pete said, rousing himself to consider the world outside him.

'I'd never sleep now, and besides, it's dawn. Come out and look at it. We get a wonderful view from here.'

The first grey light had gone and colour had returned to the world. High summer had spangled the hedges with roses, flung riotous heads of meadowsweet into the ditches, made vivid the little wood beyond the garden, where every hue from silver green through emerald and olive shaded to the near black of a solitary cypress spiralling into a sky that was pearled with remote cloud, which the sun tinged with a soft radiance that was softer than the palest rose, yet glowed with colour.

The hill dropped away below them, folded and creased, and, in every crack and rift, humped summer-splendid trees flickered their leaves in barely perceptible shivering movement, so that the landscape quivered beneath them, changing as the light strengthened. Rose deepened to scarlet, and the small puffed clouds grew and darkened.

Far below, the waters of Horton Mere took the image of the sky, so that the world stood on its head, sky beneath, glowing in the stillness of the scarcely riffled lake.

The heather was dark and clumped, the glim of unopened buds masking it with pale lilac, and beyond the Mere the bracken-clad fells stretched to the far horizon, mottled by the moving woolly backs of sheep that were as shapeless as the grey boulders, and indistinguishable until they moved.

A lorry ground up the hill, shattering the silence. They listened as it cornered, gears screeching, and then the sound faded slowly into the distance, audible for a time that seemed interminable.

Only after it had gone was Pete aware that the birds were chanting their morning praise, the faint first note taken up and echoed until all around them blackbird and thrush and sparrow, blue tit and lark and chaffinch were calling, the sound melodious, in contrast to the yakkering of the magpies that nested in a tall tree that grew out of the old brick wall surrounding the garden, and in the raucous mockery that was the crows' welcome to the sun.

Pete looked at the view. It was familiar, and yet unfamiliar, for it was his daily portion, but he had never seen it from this angle, nor had he, before, had time to stand and stare at the light, wondering at its quality and at the clarity of air that showed Jasper's cows moving as they grazed, and a hare hurtling at the top of its speed up the little track that was its familiar homeward path when day shattered the secrecy of night.

If only he could stand for ever and think of nothing.

Instead he turned back to the kitchen, with Sheila at his heels, busy with her own thoughts. She began to lay breakfast for the children, working with the speed of long-standing familiarity, not needing to think about her task at all.

The surgery door shut. The sound startled both of them. Sheila turned expectantly, waiting for Dai, whose weary footsteps sounded heavily on the linoleum that covered the passage floor.

Pete dared not question the Vet. He sat, waiting, his eyes asking for the news that his voice could not demand. Sheila made coffee, and passed a cup to her husband, also, wordlessly, asking for re-assurance.

Dai dropped into the old arm-chair that stood near the Aga. The white cat, newly returned from hunting, jumped to her master's lap. She was soon to have kittens, and she stretched herself and turned and twisted, unable to find comfort, yet wanting Dai's knee.

Dai took a sip at his coffee. It was scalding hot, but he needed it badly. He was so tired that he could barely keep his eyes from shutting. It was an effort to lift the cup, to try and think of words, to open his mouth and speak. He drank again.

'The dog will be all right,' he said.

Pete stared at him, unable to credit the words, unable to believe that the nightmare was ended, that the dog would live and run and play with Johnny again.

Dai put down his cup. Within seconds he was sound asleep. It had been a long and difficult night, and twice he despaired of victory, but the dog was strong and also lucky, for Tanner could not have laid a lethal dose. All the same, it had been a close thing. He woke briefly, and looked up at Pete, intending to say these thoughts, but the effort was too much. He slept again.

'Can I take the dog?' Pete asked.

'I'd leave him for a bit. I'll ask Dai when he wakes.' She glanced at the clock, at the second hand chasing round, speeding the minutes away. 'It's only a short while to surgery time. He never gets enough sleep. I'll ring and let you know. Will you be at home?'

'I'll be with Johnny,' Pete said, suddenly stimulated, and raced outside, coasting in the Land Rover down the hill a short way. He did not want to wake Dai with its engine. He whistled all the way home.

CHAPTER FOURTEEN

JOHNNY spent most of the night awake, staring at the ceiling, his expression so bleak that he worried Rosie. She sent her mother back to bed, and sat beside her small brother, leaving the light to chase away shadows for both of them.

Johnny did not answer when she spoke. He seemed to have withdrawn into a dark world of his own. She wished he would scream or cry, or behave in some way that was more normal.

If the dog died. . . .

She fell asleep as dawn silvered the sky and then transformed it to rose. Beside her, Johnny turned his head, watched clouds brushed with colour, saw a blackbird preen in the tree outside his window, heard the call of a cock-pheasant in the coppice, and yet did not hear them at all. Instead a small insistent voice inside his head repeated, 'Rex. Rex. Rex.'

He heard his father come into the house. He did not want to see him, did not want to see anyone, did not want to hear the words that he knew must come. He looked up as Pete came into the room, and the farmer felt a knot in his throat when he saw the child's eyes.

'Rex is all right, Johnny!' he said urgently, leaning over the bed, taking the boy's small hot hands in his. 'Rex is all right. I'm going to bring him home soon, when he's had a rest.'

It was almost an hour before Johnny's sobs died away and he fell asleep. During the whole time Pete held him, not knowing what to say, or do, and wondering through what nightmare abyss the child had passed in the long cold hours of dark.

The shrilling telephone bell woke both of them. Pete moved stiffly. His son lay against his shoulder, and he himself was half in the chair, half on the bed, one leg asleep, his arm cramped and his neck feeling as if it would never be straight again.

Rosie called from the bottom of the stairs.

'You can get Rex now.'

'Bring him up to me,' Johnny said anxiously, and Pete promised. It would do the dog as much good as the boy, he was sure, and Moira would have to allow it, just the once more.

Johnny could not eat. He played with the egg that Rosie boiled for him, and lay listening to the sound of vehicles past his window. The old tractor from Windy Hollow, the whine of the gears of the lorry that came for the churns at Wellans, the sharp rip of tyres as the cattle cake man braked in the yard, Sam barking defiance at him, hating him, no one knew why.

It seemed hours before the familiar sound of his father's Land Rover engine came to him. He sat up, expectant.

Pete found the dog limp and exhausted, but well enough to wag his draggle-plumed tail, and astonishingly, to bestow a lick on the man's hand. Rex had learned in the long hours of night that men could help him. In that new knowledge a trust was born that embraced Dai and Pete, and in time extended to Jasper and Ned. Everyone else he treated with tolerant condescension, allowing no liberties, but showing neither dislike nor fear.

Pete, lifting him, was thankful that the dog had ceased to distrust him. It would make life much simpler. The collie wagged his tail again, and his brown eyes looked as if they were trying to convey a message. He lifted his head and licked Pete's face.

By the time Pete had come indoors Johnny was half-way down the stairs, one hand trying to keep his pyjama trousers in place. They were made from an old pair of Tony's, and Rosie had put elastic in the waist. She had mismeasured, and they had always been too big.

'Back to bed, or you won't see Rex,' Pete said, keeping his face straight, not wanting to show how relieved he was to find Johnny well enough to want to get out of bed. The child had been content to lie still and sleep for most of the past few days, and on his first day up had been listless.

Johnny raced back at almost his usual speed and jumped under the covers. Pete put the dog on the bed. The collie was weak, but his tail waved in wild joy, beating against the chair back, sweeping into Pete's face, and Johnny, after one incredulous look, put his arms round the dog and held him as if he could never bear to let him go again.

'Rex thought I wasn't here. That's why he runned away,' Johnny said, making what was almost his only mistake, one that the family corrected time and time again. 'He won't do it any more.'

When Moira came up with Johnny's morning milk she found him sound asleep, with the dog, equally fast asleep, lying beside him on the bed. Acknowledging temporary defeat, she put the glass on the bedside table, and went away. Half an hour later Rex woke. He was hungry and, smelling nourishment, he drank every drop, and then stretched himself comfortably on the bed and fell asleep again, white droplets beading his long whiskers.

That night, in the *Swan*, the men were bitter. Tanner, had he been telepathic, would have had burning ears, as half the villagers had tales to tell against him.

Ned Foley owed him a grudge for setting snares which were crueller to the beasts than any that the old man had seen, crueller even than those that Brook Holler, the recluse beyond Horton Pike, set for the hares.

'Had a dog poisoned myself, three weeks back,' Jo Needler said despondently. Life always too much for him, too full of sorrows, of one thing after another, of children with mumps and measles and bronchitis and croup, a wife with a back that ached nine days out of ten and made her creep about, crotchety, nothing like the pert miss he'd married. Slugs and snails and blackfly and green fly, onion fly and carrot fly, and flies he had never seen before or even heard of, came to plague his nursery garden. When the flies did not come hordes of caterpillars descended like locusts, so that crops never came up to expectation, and bills remained unpaid, and his wife's mouth grew tight and grim, and the children fed badly and sneezed and snuffled, while the washing hung in damp festoons all over the house.

'Gave it a dose of salt as soon as I saw what was wrong, but didn't do no good. Lucky it wasn't Painter.' Painter had fulfilled his early promise, and was leader of the pack that the Huntsman groomed, each man bringing his own hound, each hound well cared for, fed on the best meat, and prized by his owner. Jo had paid one or two bills by backing Painter on a trail.

'Time we did summat about Tanner,' Ned grumbled, blowing froth towards Fleck who caught it on his nose, and sat grinning, an idiotic laughing expression bringing amused applause from the men seated nearby, applause that Fleck revelled in, being a clown who always played to an audience. He stood up thoughtfully, anxious to keep some of the attention, and walked to Mrs. Jones and begged, looking up pleadingly at her, so that she laughed and gave him a mouthful of potato crisps which he crunched noisily. He barked once, his thanks being demanded by Ned, who had early discovered that his dog had circus manners, and then, tail beating merrily, he returned to Ned's feet. Finding attention lapsed again he pawed anxiously at Jo Needler, until the man gave a sheepish grin and shook the proffered paw.

'Come on, boy, shake my hand then,' the Huntsman said, and Fleck solemnly obliged, but suddenly tired of the ploy and returned to sit pressed close against his master's leg, his ears pricking as each man spoke.

'Can't you charge Tanner, Pete?' asked Rob Hinney, the cowman from Wellans. He had red-rimmed eyes, fighting to keep awake, dropping tired after a night spent with one of the Wellans' Jerseys, the calf born at dawn and a deep mystery at that for how did Rosina, pretty pale Jersey cream, and pedigree bred for years, and Emperor, whose pedigree he had checked only last night, come to produce a little red and white calf that looked all Ayrshire?

Rob had worried about it for hours and gone back three times to check lest his eyes were playing tricks, but there it was and Ted as mystified as he was, but not Rosina, why should she care, a calf to lick and prize and cherish, no matter what colour. Strange to be an animal, Rob mused, not

116

knowing that he could slide as easy as butter into the skin of a cow, think like a cow, guess what was worrying a cow, frightening her, teasing her, prevent trouble before it came.

Pete did it with dogs, but not yet with Rex. Rex was alien to him, bred wild, not home-bred, knowing things that his other dogs did not know, things about the night-time world on the high hills, sudden death from the chasing owl, the rat-trap fox-jaws, the wiles of the wind sighing above the rabbit burrows, the stir of grass in the deep dark, the look of a crescent moon in the midnight sky, the pleasure of baying to the full moon, alone on the misty fells.

Rex was not a tame dog yet, too much had happened to him, too many memories had shaped him, so that he would run from a fox, remembering death when he was a pup, and not chase it, not till the urge to save his sheep over-rode the puppyhood terror. Pete knew none of this and could not make allowances for it, was baffled by the dog, not yet in tune with him.

Johnny, having only instinct to guide him, and the need for companionship to lead him on, was all dog himself when he was with Rex and had no need for translation. Civilization had barely touched him, nor yet moulded him, so that he too knew the need to run on the hills, the urge to chase and play, the sudden wind-induced madness that made animals and school children run riot and drove school teachers wild as the mob spirit, wind-crazed, took over for the day.

Ned knew this and thought about it, watching the men bandy words, content to sit and drink slow, and dip his finger in his beer for Fleck to lick, and stroke the dog's smooth coat, and see how Painter lifted his head when a log slid from the fire, and the Huntsman's Siamese cat, from his refuge high on the dresser, never closed his blue squint eyes, but watched with half-flattened ears, and now and again swore his warning as a dog lifted its head and stared at him.

Ben Timmins, off duty, and dry after a day spent in petty doing-nothing, came through the door, and grinned at the Huntsman.

'Pint of bitter. And quick, Huntsman, I'm dry as Horton Beck in summertime.'

'Looking for crime, Ben?' asked Rob Hinney with a yawn, still puzzling over his little red calf.

'Got any to report?' Ben asked. He was a big man, a slow man, with his own ways of coping on his little patch. A glare from Ben and a sharp word did as much good to a youngster scrumping apples as a shaking from his parent, putting the fear of the Law into him, stopping uncivilized instincts at birth. Few boys dared out-face Ben Timmins, only the Tanner lads, and they were like their father, all from the same foul nest.

'Dunno. Not seen an Ayrshire bull in my cow field?' Rob asked incautiously, and provoked a roar of laughter.

'Cows giving cross-breds then, Rob?' asked Pete, with a grin. 'Not Ted's pedigrees going off the rails?'

'I dunno,' Rob said, regretting his words already, but aware that unless he sold the calf now it would stick out like a swan in a hen run. 'Rosina had a red and white calf last night, and that's a black mystery to me.'

'A red and white mystery if you ask me,' Mrs. Jones said, laughing. 'Be like that Friesian of Josh Johnson's. Bred to a bull from the Centre, and she had a red and white calf too, about a year back. There was some mighty hurried checking on the old bull, I can tell you.'

'Maybe it's a germ, Rob,' Ben Timmins said, his beer half gone, and an expression of extreme content on his bronze-red face.

'New disease among Jerseys,' added the Huntsman.

'Hope it don't spread,' Rob said unhappily, half serious, always slow to see a leg pull. 'Have to check on the herd. We bought Rosina after our own lot had foot and mouth. Wonder how far back her pedigree goes.'

'Be the bull's pedigree, surely,' Pete said, and then went on, his mind busy with other things. 'Ben, how do we stand with Tanner? He's laid strychnine again, and my sheepdog picked up the poison.'

'Sure it was Tanner?' Ben asked.

'Pretty sure. Who else would it be?' Pete knew of no one else likely to be so daft, but Ben was always cautious.

'Laid it on your land, did he? Did you see him?'

'Not on my land. Dog went off,' Pete said, wondering what

that had to do with it.

'Well, now.' Ben crossed his legs, and looked thoughtfully into the fire as if he thought it would give him inspiration. 'Dog was straying, right?'

Pete nodded.

'That's against the law in sheep country, and you ought to know that, Pete. Your fault there. And dog was straying on Tanner's land, so he was trespassing. And if Tanner lays strychnine on his own ground, well it's anti-social, and daft as well, with his own creatures there, but unless you can prove he laid it where other animals were in danger, out in the ditch in the lane, which is public, for instance, there's not a thing you can do. Not going to try and sue him, are you? Wouldn't stand a chance in a court of law.'

'Nothing we can do, then?' Jo Needler asked. He'd have to make certain Painter never strayed if that was the case. Not always easy to make sure the animals were in, especially if there was a bitch nearby. Never an end to the difficulties, Jo thought, and new ones all the time. As soon as you'd settled on one thing, there was another to take its place. Like battling against twitch grass, roots everywhere unseen and the stuff coming up again and again to plague you.

'Nothing. I'll have a word with Tanner, try and get him to use one of the new poisons, or to employ the ratman. No sense in endangering his own stock but you know Tanner, and him and me's not the best of friends.'

The men grinned. Ben had made the understatement of the year, for he was as welcome at Tanner's as a thunder-storm in harvest time.

'Been to any trials lately, Pete?' Ben asked, to change the subject.

Pete shook his head.

'Moira gets fed up with me off every Saturday and her with all the work to do. Not worth it too often. Might try again next year with Johnny's pup. He shapes nicely with the sheep, but as yet he's disobedient, and can't risk that.'

Can't risk him running off to find Johnny come after-school-time either, Pete thought, draining his last pint while Bet watched him, aware, as if she read his thoughts, that it would soon be time to go. Wonder if Rex'd leave to go home from a place fifty miles away: it was not a welcome worry and it flicked into his brain, leaving a niggling anxiety. Looked as if the damned pup was never going to be worth much as a sheepdog. Mean gettting rid of him and buying a decent biddable animal. And then what would Johnny do? Damn it to hell, Pete thought viciously, as he emptied the last drops and stood up.

'Johnny better?' asked Ben.

'He's coming on. Been proper seedy,' Pete answered, shrugging into his coat. 'Dog being poisoned didn't help.'

'I've got something for Johnny,' Ned said, remembering suddenly, and took a small tobacco tin out of his pocket. He opened it to show Pete.

It was full of artificial flies, minute, lifelike, made from bits of brilliant feather, green and blue and scarlet, patched with yellow, they glinted in the light, legs and wings and feelers, magical, almost real.

'He'll be right proud of those, Ned. Thanks,' Pete said, stowing them away.

'Promised to show him how to fish wi 'em,' Ned added incautiously, standing up in his turn, with Fleck eager beside him.

'In whose bit of river, Ned?' the policeman asked, his grin broad, he and Ned knowing each other well and not always meeting on the right side of the Law either. 'I'll be watching for you when Johnny's around again.'

'This time I've got me a licence,' Ned said, triumphant, pulling the trophy from his pocket and exhibiting it as if it were a first edition or the winning cheque on a football pool. 'I wouldn't teach Johnny bad ways,' he added virtuously.

The men laughed disbelievingly, but Ben looked at him curiously.

'You old sinner, I don't believe you would either,' he said at last, and added yet another footnote to his vast store of wisdom based on the oddities of human nature, as seen in the course of his official duties.

CHAPTER FIFTEEN

REX was a sober dog when he recovered from the poisoning. He remained weak for several days, during which he spent most of his time asleep on the straw in the outhouse. Twice each day he was taken to see Johnny, who was recovering rapidly and bored and naughty, hating the tedium of convalescence. Moira was exhausted by him, and began to resent the affection that he bestowed on the collie while treating her with irritable rudeness and downright disobedience.

By the time school began again in September, both Johnny and Rex were fit, and the dog spent his days with Sam and Bet out in the fields. The routine was broken for a short while when Bet had her third litter, and Rex had to take her place. He herded skilfully, obedient to the sound of Pete's whistle and his flicking fingers, and quicker than Sam to bring the flock to order. Sam was much better at singling individual sheep. This was a skill that Rex had yet to master. He preferred to see the flock in a solid mass, with no outliers breaking the satisfying block of crowded bodies.

Pete was pleased with the dog's progress except for one thing. No matter what they were doing, or how far from home, the clock that worked inside Rex's brain told him that Johnny was coming home from school and he streaked away, over the rough fields, clearing wall and hedge and ditch in a headlong effort to be at the gate to greet the child. In the end Pete acknowledged defeat and sent the dog off, rather than be forced to endure constant disobedience. No matter what he did, he could not keep Rex with him when Johnny was due. Once he tried tying him, but the collie went berserk, straining and pulling at the chain until he began to choke, and then, giving up, sat down and howled until Pete released him, and he vanished in a wild spurt in order to reach home before his small master arrived.

Bet's puppies, in which Sam, who had fathered them, took a mild interest, were a source of fascination to Rex. He and Johnny visited them daily, and while Johnny prepared their food after they had been weaned, Rex climbed in to the compartment that Pete had made for them in the shed and sat with them, while Bet raced out for a short spell of freedom, exultantly, free from responsibilities.

The young collie was endlessly patient, allowing the pups to roll over him and bite his tail, and he missed them when they had been sold, and, with Bet, went hunting round the farm, puzzled by their disappearance.

A second Christmas came and went, and winter gripped the fells. Ice dammed the streams, and long icicles fell from the ledges and ridges, the rushing water frozen in its pride. Ian and Pete trudged the fells in frequent misery, watching over the ewes, anxious that nothing should go wrong before lambing time. They carried extra food to them, the grass being sparse and unnourishing. Both were surly and tired, and even the dogs longed for the warmth of the outhouse, and their night time meal.

Rex, coming home at three-thirty every day, was always hungry, and Moira had to take care that he did not slip into the kitchen and steal any meat that she left lying around. She began to hate him, both for his thieving ways, and for the attention that Johnny gave him. She might as well not exist when the dog was there, and Johnny only came indoors when it was too dark to stay in the yard.

Rex was now full-grown, and though not yet as solidly muscled as Sam, was a splendid dog, having an eager head, mobile inquisitive ears, eyes that subdued the boldest sheep and sent her, half hypnotized, back with the flock, and a sleek, lovely line from his head, along his back, to his plumed tail, so that when he crouched on the grass, or slid forward behind the flock, he moved with easy grace, quick-silver fluid in his movement.

Johnny was only coaxed out of bed by the barking dog.

The child hated the icy mornings, when frost rimed his windows in intricate patterns, and he had to dress in the bitter cold. If his mother were not up, he slipped down to the kitchen and dressed by the warm Aga, his father and Ian saying nothing as they drank scalding coffee and ate hunks of bread with their bacon, putting off the moment when they must brave the cold. Moira would not have the child coddled, and if she were about he had to dress quickly, and then run downstairs to get warm.

The hill was always icy, and he slipped and skidded to school, meeting the other children in the schoolyard where they made slides and sped along them in headlong excitement. It was an old school, built when Victoria was still young. Its boiler creaked and groaned, and the pipes were often cold. At other times water bubbled and seethed in them and little spurts of steam escaped through the valves.

That winter the washbasins were all frozen, and the children went home filthy, and for the first time in his life the schoolmaster was glad that their only facilities were chemical, and not water closets that would also freeze and crack.

On the coldest day of the year, the ancient boiler lay down and died. The children, arriving at school, found the heat had entirely vanished, and the schoolmaster was waiting at the door to greet each one, make sure he had folk at home, and send him back again.

Johnny, walking home reluctantly, past the *Swan*, saw Ranger, and went through the open door to greet him. He had never been inside the inn. It was a grown-up place, a place for the men who came there after a long day's work, a place that was taboo in licensing hours, and only recently allowable to Ian, who was, in Johnny's eyes, quite grown-up himself, but had still a few months to go to his nineteenth birthday.

'Skipping school, Johnny?' The Huntsman asked in surprise, seeing the boy kneeling on the floor, patting Ranger, who thumped an enraptured stern, and attempted to wash the child cleaner than he had ever been in his life. 'Give over, Ranger. You'll eat him away!'

Johnny laughed.

'The boiler's burst. We've been sent home,' he said, look-ing, fascinated, at the vast black timbered room, the huge scrubbed table and the dark settles, the earthenware jugs hanging from the rafters, the two-gallon copper kettle, shining on the hob, puffing small spurts of steam into the air, and the bright rag rug on which lay the cat, nursing her fourteenth litter, her claws flexing with pleasure while the kittens tugged at her. Johnny, seeing her, was beside her in a second.

'Mum not expecting you home, then?' asked Mrs. Jones, appearing suddenly, like Judy in a Punch and Judy show, from the far side of the table, where she had been on her knees scrubbing the flags.

Johnny, his fingers gentle on a kitten's soft back, shook his head.

'Then I'd think there might be time to get warm before you go up the hill, then,' the Huntsman said. His small brown face crinkled merrily at the boy. The Huntsman liked children. He rarely saw his own grandchildren, living far away in London.

'Might be something in that cupboard too,' said Mrs. Jones, wiping her hands on her apron as she walked towards the old black oak cupboard against the far wall. Above it hung a mottled jug, on which words were printed. Johnny looked at it curiously.

'What does that say?' he asked, one eye on the jug and one on Mrs. Jones, who was bringing out fruit cake and scones and ginger biscuits.

'Never made out the proper order,' the Huntsman said, looking up at it. 'But it says on each little panel ...

> 'He who buys land buys stones ...
> He who buys flesh buys bones ...
> He who buys eggs buys many shells ...
> He who buys good ale buys nothing else ...'

'It's funny,' Johnny decided, not quite understanding it, and by now more interested in the fruit cake which was making his mouth water. He climbed up on to the big chair.

'Will Cat let me hold a kitten?'

'Shouldn't be surprised,' the Huntsman said, picking up the tiniest while the cat watched with half-closed, sleepy eyes, used to people who liked to nurse her babies. Johnny took the tiny thing gently, lips half-parted, eyes wide with wonder that anything so small and soft could be alive, and able to run and move and feed. It made the tiniest purr, and he was delighted.

'It likes me,' he said.

'Coffee or hot orange?' the Huntsman asked. 'Too cold for a cold drink.'

Johnny chose orange, and watched, intrigued, as the Huntsman sliced pieces off a lemon and an apple, and then added a cherry on a stick.

'Fruit cocktail,' he said, laughing, and winked at Mrs. Jones. 'Don't tell your Mum.'

Eating the biggest slice of fruit cake he had ever seen, Johnny contemplated the room, the beer mugs on the long trestle against the wall, the corner where they pulled the beer, the overhanging unfamiliar cloying smell.

'I don't think I'd like beer,' he observed, his nose wrinkling, and Jasper, coming into the room, his coat huddled round him against the cold, blew on his hands and laughed.

'I'd hope not,' he said, solemnly. 'Rich drinking for a six-year-old, and take all your pocket money, too, young Johnny. Bad habit, isn't it, Huntsman?'

'Very bad for a young'un,' the Huntsman agreed, watching Nell greet Ranger regally, then nose the kittens, which she loved, and sit down and look up at Johnny who held out his own small fist and shook her uplifted paw.

'Never offers it to anyone else,' Jasper said. 'It's funny. She does go for anything young. Came to see if you'd any spare eggs,' he added. 'Bess's hens seem to 'ave gone on strike. Don't like the weather.'

'Does anyone?' Mrs. Jones asked, taking brown eggs from an earthenware bowl on the dresser. 'I can spare a few. Settle up later, Jasper. I've not got change.'

'Coming my way, young Johnny?' Jasper asked.

Johnny wiped the crumbs from his mouth with the back of his hand and stood up reluctantly. There would be nothing to do at home, and Rex was out with his father. The dog would never come to meet him at this time of day. And Mum might not have any dinner for him, a prospect that he contemplated with sudden dismay. Best get there quick so she knew he was coming.

He went out with Jasper into an icy wind that took their breath away and snarled bitter fingers in Nell's thick coat so that even she felt cold and shivered.

'Watch your step, young'un,' Jasper warned. 'Near slipped meself coming down the hill. Couldn't do with a broken leg at my age ... or at your age come to that.'

It was too cold to talk. Too cold to do more than endure, to feel the wind sneaking into scarlet icy ears, probing through thick clothes, making noses run and eyes smart and fingers and toes ache in protest, until walking was sheer misery, and every step hurt.

Pete, expecting snow, as a warmer spell was forecast, had brought the sheep from the tops down to the field close to the farm. The dogs were with him, their work almost done. Bet was bringing home the stragglers, Sam was singling an ailing ewe that needed warmth for a few days, and Rex was waiting, his tongue hanging out, standing beside the farmer.

His quick ears, always alert, heard Johnny's voice, as the boy walked up the hill beside Jasper, and made a sudden remark. Johnny! Rex looked up at Pete, but the man had heard nothing, and all his attention was on the other two dogs. Bet brought in the last four stragglers, and Pete shut the gate, just in time to see Rex clear the wall, and slide pell mell into the lane.

'Rex!' he yelled, furious, wondering what on earth had got into the dog, vowing that this time he'd teach the brute a lesson he would never forget. It was high time the beast learnt obedience, and this time he was not going to meet Johnny, unless he was heading for the school, and then there would be trouble. He jumped on to the wall, to see if he could discover why the dog had run off, and stayed there, completely paralysed.

Jim Betwick had called at Wellans to take Sue out for the day. Sue had not been ready, they were late, and Jim was making up for lost time. Foot down, he flung the car along the icy road until even Sue protested.

'We're late, and it's your fault,' he said savagely. Patience had never been a habit with him.

Pete saw the car speeding towards him, down the lane. He could see the lane, see the ice, see Johnny and Nell and Jasper, plodding up the hill, in the middle of the road, far below him and out of ear-shot. As the car flashed by he yelled, but Jim did not hear. He wanted to get to the country club beyond Lancaster in time for lunch.

Pete stood with his fist clenched. Terror made his legs soft as lambswool. He could not bear to watch yet could not look away. He saw the car take the corner, saw Rex come flashing from the hedge and hurl himself at Johnny, saw the child sprawl into the ditch with the dog on top of him, saw Nell turn to Jasper and put her paws on his shoulder and try to push him out of the way and saw the pair of them vanish as the little red car spun on its wheels, hit the wall, skidded back to the road, took the second corner, and then overturned, hitting the wall again, its wheels still spinning as they tore at the empty air.

Only then did he manage to move. He jumped, landed with a thud that jarred ankles and back, and ran, feet slipping on the glazed surface, boots pounding, his own heart thudding, fighting waves of sickness. What had happened to Jasper, and Nell, and dear God, let Johnny be all right. Let Johnny be all right.

Johnny was bruised and grazed and filthy, he was covered in blood, but when Pete examined him it was not his blood. The bumper of the car had torn a large patch of fur and muscle from the dog's shoulder, and Johnny, holding his collie tightly, was steeped in Rex's blood.

He had not seen Jasper or Nell, Pete was sure. He had no need to look at either, no need to wonder if the old man needed a doctor, or the dog a Vet. Nell lay across her master, her head on his shoulder. The two heads were unharmed, except for a streak of dirt across Jasper's dead face. Neither had to suffer the loss of the other, Pete thought numbly, as he bent over Johnny and carried the child and the dog round the corner and out of sight of the holocaust.

He did not know what to do. He did not know if the occupants of the car were alive, and if he went to telephone another car might pile into the scarlet roadster, which had crashed on a blind corner. Johnny was too shaken to go home alone, and too worried about his dog. One thing, it would stop him asking about Jasper.

'Johnny, will you wait here for me, and promise not to move? Keep Rex very still. He's all right, but that's a nasty cut and it mustn't get dirty.' It might just work, he thought. It might just keep the child from coming to see where I am. He put his coat round the boy, and whistled to Sam and Bet who were watching anxiously from over the wall, having run through the fields to keep up with him.

'Stay with Johnny,' he ordered, and the dogs sat obediently. Bet put her head down to greet Rex, and then sniffing his shoulder, set herself to wash the gaping wound clean.

'She won't hurt it,' Pete said, and summoned his courage to go back and look at the occupants of the car. He went to move Jasper and Nell, but thought he had better leave them where they lay for the police to see. He was not sure what he ought to do. But the couple in the car might be alive. He might be able to help. His brain span, busily and uselessly.

He leaned down and looked inside. Sue was lying sideways, but she was breathing. He could not see what damage had been done to her, and he dared not try and shift her without help. No one would ever help Jim Betwick again. His side of the car had crashed into the wall. Pete stumbled away, feeling sicker than he had ever felt in his life. Someone would have to fetch Ted, and someone would have to tell Jim's father.

He went back to Johnny, who was white-faced and shivering. He ought to take the child home, but Moira would be out shopping. Suddenly he remembered Ian, who had been with him earlier on. Where the devil was he now? He called Bet.

'Find Ian,' he said, not hopeful, but feeling it was worth a try.

She gave him an astonished glance, and then vaulted the wall, her paws scraping the slatey tiles that edged it.

Pete lit his pipe, keeping his eyes on the lane below him, his ears listening for the sound of an engine on the hill above. He could see the massed woolly backs of the sheep feeding on hay that had been strewn for them, the grey surface of Horton Mere, thralled in ice, the frost-rimed shrubbery growths at the road edges, the bright breast of a robin, pecking at a few berries on the wild rose. Would Bet find Ian, and if she did, would he have the sense to follow her?

'There's a car coming,' Johnny said, his teeth chattering so much that Pete could scarcely distinguish the words.

It was Dai's battered red Land Rover. The Vet saw them and drew into the side of the lane and stopped, climbing down to come over breathlessly and peer at Johnny.

'What on earth?'

'Take a look round the corner,' Pete said tonelessly, knowing it was brutal without warning, but not wanting to upset the child. Dai glanced at him, mystified, and walked on.

His face was set when he came back, his mouth grim, his eyes completely without expression.

'I'll take Johnny home and phone from there,' he said.

'Moira's out. Place is empty,' Pete felt matters were beyond him and far too complicated. He was aware of a thin whimpering noise from the car.

'Sheila's home and Rex needs attention. Johnny can stay with us until you come for him. Why aren't you at school, Johnny?' he asked, and Pete realized that he had not even had time to ponder that question.

'The boiler's burst,' Johnny said. He was feeling sick. He had hit his side against the road when Rex jumped at him, and been terrified by the dog's behaviour until he heard the speeding wheels. 'Rex saved me from being run over.'

'He's a brave dog,' Dai said, and added quickly, 'That's not a bad hurt. Let's go home and get you warm, Johnny. Into the back with you both. There's something there that will help you keep cosy, and a big blanket.'

The baby donkey lifted a curious head as Johnny was pushed in beside it.

'His mother's dead, and we're going to try and feed him on a bottle. You and Rex O.K.?'

Johnny nodded. The dog licked his face as he curled up on the floor, his interest taken by the tiny blue-eyed foal that lay there so quietly. Dai put the big old rug over him. It smelled comforting, redolent of dog and cat and calf and sheep.

Sheila was busy with her two younger children, both sent home from school and both bored and already quarrelling. She had just set them to making a zoo out of modelling clay while she fed the animals when the Land Rover came into the yard.

Dai jumped down.

'Johnny's in the back with Rex. Jim Betwick almost ran into him.'

'Thank God he didn't,' Sheila said, and then saw her husband's face.

'He's killed himself and Jasper and Nell and God knows what he's done to Sue.'

Sheila could not bear to look at him. There was a tight feeling in her throat and it was hard not to let tears flood her eyes as she thought of Jasper, and of Nell, seeing the two of them for a vivid moment as she had seen them when Jasper came last to the surgery and Nell sat patiently at his feet, waiting her turn without whining or pulling as many other dogs did, and then jumped obediently on to the table for Dai to examine her. Jasper had not been told the dog had a malignant growth. There was some time before it would harm any organ, but operation was hopeless. Jasper would have been heartbroken. Perhaps it was as well they had died together.

It still left desolation. Sheila lifted Johnny, who clung to her, shivering.

'Jasper and Nell are dead,' he said.

Sheila stared at him.

'How do you know?'

'I saw,' Johnny said. 'Before Dad took me away. Rex is hurt too,' he added, accepting death, knowing it well from farm experience, too worried about his dog to grieve for Jasper, not yet old enough to realize human death and finality.

'You look as if *you* are,' Sheila had pushed away the

blanket, and saw that his chin was bruised, and his coat smothered in blood.

'Rex is hurt, not me.' The dog limped awkwardly to the tail of the Land Rover. Sheila put Johnny down and lifted the collie. The three of them went into the house, just as Dai came running out again, picked up the baby donkey, and hurried with it into the kitchen before driving off, his face even grimmer.

He reached the corner to find Pete talking to the policeman, the dogs beside him. Ian was standing beside the little car, trying to comfort Sue, who had returned to awareness, but, although she begged them to get her out, Ben Timmins refused to try. He wanted the ambulance men, who knew how to set about lifting her. It was obvious that her leg was broken, if nothing else. She was lying on her side, and even if they did help her out, she would have to be laid in the road. A squad car was coming from the town. It couldn't come quick enough for Ben, who had never seen such an accident before in his life, not with all the victims folk he'd known, some of them, like Jasper, for ever, and young Sue and Jim, who he'd watched grow up. It was a bad job, he thought inadequately, and gave a deep sigh of relief as he heard the ambulance bell.

It was quiet in the *Swan* that night. Death had come close, and stroked each one of them with numbing fingers. The shiver of reality, of unseen mysteries beyond the edge of fear, was with every man, chastening his thoughts and silencing his tongue.

The empty chair in the chimney corner, that had been Jasper's by right of long use, the memory of Nell, with her proud head and wise shining eyes and ever-ready welcoming tail, hung among them so that even the hounds were subdued, sensing gloom among their masters, unaware of the cause, yet respecting their mood.

Mrs. Jones had a lump in her throat and trouble keeping her eyes dry and no word or smile for anyone. She had liked old Jasper, understood his crustiness, shared his pleasure in a good Hunt well run, and appreciated his kindliness. True, he was old, and had not long to go, and death had come swiftly and mercifully, but he would be on Sue's conscience for the rest of her life, along with the boy who had killed him. It was a bad job.

Ted, his mouth bitter, had come in for a drink, and reported briefly on his daughter, who had a broken leg and two cracked ribs and slight concussion, and did not mention that she was completely hysterical and her mental condition gave cause for more worry than her physical state. He left his drink half touched, finding that even there there was no consolation. He flicked his fingers to his dog, and went up to the fells, walking through the dark with savage desperation, as if trying to outpace his own thoughts.

'Won't be the same without Jasper,' Ned said, missing Jasper more than most, and voicing every man's thought. The words lay on the air in the firelit timbered room, a fitter epitaph than any that the vicar could devise, when, a few days later, the wind blew chill across the cemetery and earth thudded on the plain wood coffin and every man in the village took off his cap and said some kind of prayer for the old man's soul.

It was Ned who achieved ultimate desolation, burying Nell beside Jasper's other dogs, another tump on the windy moor, a tump that he could never see without a small thickening in his throat and a twinge of grief. These absurdly small memorials reminded him far more of Jasper than the silent unimaginable grave with its solemn headstone, standing, regimented, in the well-tended cemetery that seemed to Ned to have nothing whatever to do with those who lay there, lost in eternal unknowingness.

CHAPTER SIXTEEN

JOHNNY's seventh birthday fell on a Saturday, and Pete fulfilled a long-standing promise by taking him, with the sheepdogs, to the trials at Appledale. Rex was fully grown, showing signs of the powerful build that would be his in a year or so, now almost a two-year-old, and brilliant with the sheep. In spite of a tolerant affection that he had developed for Pete, he was still Johnny's dog, and nothing would make him change. Meeting Johnny was a ritual that nothing was allowed to stop. Pete was glad when the holidays came along and he could take the child on the fells, and keep the dog with him.

Often, on the first day of school, he waited to see if the dog had lost the habit, but no matter where they were, Rex still chased away, Johnny more important than any sheep. The farmer came at last to the rather odd conclusion that, for the collie, Johnny was a super sheep, to be guarded above the rest of the flock, a charge and a duty as well as a being loved beyond all other creatures. Pete was always forced to send the dog home, knowing that otherwise Rex would go off on his own, in answer to an imperative summons that must never be denied.

The trials were held in a huge sloping field that was half-way up a hill behind the town. The whole day was rapture for Johnny, from the drive through the misty dawn in the rattle-trap Land Rover, the soft top shaking in a mean sneaking wind that made Pete wonder how the field would lie, and if the dogs would find the wind so strong that they could not hear the commands given to them. It would add to the day's difficulties.

Johnny looked around the field, imitating his elders,

seeing, when his father pointed them out, the clumped trees in the middle where a bold sheep might play hide and seek and lose time, the shrubby bushes that masked the dog's view. Pete, standing beside his son, nodded to old acquaintances from Burton and Horton and Buttonskille, and from far away as well, one man coming annually from Devonshire with five dogs, two inside his smart car, and three in the boot, on straw, the boot altered with a special fitting, so that it could be propped open a few inches to allow the dogs air.

They jumped out and ran to stretch their legs, rejoicing in freedom, but coming at once to sit beside their master when he flicked a finger, and look about them with an experienced air and mouths a-laugh as if entertained by the thought that any of these rough half-trained pups could challenge their supremacy.

The field was not only sloping, but had a rock outcrop, a high crag that masked one end completely. The sheep would be released here, behind the crag, and if the dogs were sent sweeping left-hand, running in a wide arc, they would spot them at once. Sent right-hand, there was no view, and the crag barred the way.

Pete crouched down to the dogs' eye level, looking to see how the fold and crease of the ground blocked vision, realizing that none of the dogs would see well. The ground was too uneven. He began to plan his signals, while Johnny wandered with Rex at heel, looking up with a smile at remembered faces, admiring all the shepherds, smart in their navy blue Sunday-best, their bright ties, their new, good caps, kept only for such occasions, and the fancy crooks, this one won in Wales, that one, carved with oak leaves and acorns, and twisting like a barley sugar stick, engraved with the owner's name and the place at which it was presented. It was a long Welsh name and Johnny could not pronounce it.

There were dogs of all kinds, from heavy rough-haired collies, with their coarse behaviour, bristling when they met one another, marking, every post and wheel, to the slender gentle, small-boned animals, timid except when with the sheep.

Johnny and his dog roamed the edge of the course, marked

out by ropes knotted round stakes. One large collie growled at Rex and Rex growled back, but Johnny silenced him, and a tall shepherd with beetling eyebrows that separated his forehead from his nose, looked down at the boy and grinned. His white dog, patched with black on one paw and one ear, bristled at Rex.

'That's a good dog you've got there, son.'

Johnny grinned back, grown-up, man to man, immensely taken with himself.

'He's a wonderful dog with the sheep,' he said in the tone his father used and was startled at the roar of laughter from the men around him, tickled at his pint-sized importance.

There were many things to watch, and Johnny roved in wonder, seeing the late entries coming with their fee money, a man taking it, sitting on the solid metal bumper of a twelve-seater Land Rover, a biscuit tin on the ground beside him, full of change, the notes wadded into a rubber band in his wallet, the names written down, each one entered with the dog's name first, and then the man's. Johnny listened.

So many different dogs. Sweep, Moss, Pat, Sam, Hemp, Toss, Nan, Nell, Fly, Bet, Rip, Tag. Easy names to call across a sheepfield. Simple names, used for sheepdogs over the centuries, ever since man had discovered that a dog could help him and make his task easier. Only the dogs made sheep keeping on fell and mountain possible, for the dog ran fifty miles to a man's ten, chasing, herding, fetching, always moving, busy, willing and enjoying every second of the work.

The judge walked down the line of parked cars, stopping for a word here, and a greeting there, slow with dignity and age. Johnny thought that he had never seen a man so old. Older surely even than Jasper. Jasper would have liked to be here, he thought, remembering the old man with sudden affection, and remote regret. He stared, fascinated, at the judge, in his sombre Church elder's clothes, the sober black suit, the quiet tie, the old man's tortoise neck, wrinkled and scraggy, and the old, old face, paper-lidded eyes hooded and brooding, thin white hair clinging to the extreme edges of the bald head, as he lifted his cap to the ladies, courteous with the manners of an older generation, bowing slightly to them as he passed.

He must be over a hundred, old as Methuselah, thought Johnny, and then lowered his eyes, abashed, as he found himself staring directly into bootblack bright little round eyes that seemed to see right into his mind.

'That's a beautiful dog you have there, son,' the old voice said, and Johnny only dared look at the gnarled hands, holding a gold watch in their little claws. 'Going to enter him?'

Johnny nodded, and Pete, coming to look for him, was surprised, for he had never seen the boy awed before, but there was something about the old man that quelled the most impertinent and brought respect, even from men like Tanner who had appeared before him when he officiated as a magistrate.

The judge walked on absently. He noted the dog, and nodded to Pete, who was familiar to him. The old man wondered why he had not seen Pete for so long at the local trials. It was cold on the field, in spite of the time of the year, and one of the assistants drove the judge's car down to the judging site, so that he could sit in comfort out of the wind, the man with the stopwatch standing beside him, out in the cold, timing each dog, while the old judge made notes on performance, knowing more about sheepdogs than any man alive, and working wholeheartedly to better the breed and get more folk to appreciate the skill and grace of the working collie.

Johnny found the ice-cream van, and shared his cornet with Rex, breaking off small pieces to give to the dog, earning his father's disapproval. Bet and Sam sat quietly, watching the other collies, and as the first one took his place, their ears pricked, and their small bodies tensed with eagerness as the four sheep appeared on the far edge of the field. Rex stiffened and turned his head, catching the scent of sheep borne on the wind, which was blowing strongly towards the shepherd, making it difficult for the dog to hear his whistles.

The sheep came pelting, pell-mell, missing the first

hurdles, between which they had to pass. One of them broke away, bounding high, skipping across the field, and the dog, a rakish black collie with a white tip to his tail, hesitated and then broke after it, running too fast, unable, because of the wind, to hear the whistle that the shepherd used to recall him.

It was hopeless, time had gone, and the man, a hulky youngish man with tow-coloured untidy hair and a face reddened by wind and beer, shrugged, and called the dog loudly, sending him to pen the sheep in their fold at the judge's end of the field.

'Young know-nothing, doesn't even know how to train a dog,' an elderly white-moustached shepherd standing beside Pete said in disgust. 'One of the modern lot. Let the sheep into a field and look them over once a week if they're lucky, never mind maggot or foot rot, or anything else. Half the flock lame, half of them coughing, all of them wormy. Use chemicals to dose 'em, and to dip 'em, and not even know their faces, let alone their ways. That's not shepherding.'

He was next, and he went quietly to his place, crook angled in his hand. The flag waved, and he sent the dog, a sleek and slender collie bitch with gentle ways, left-handed in a sweeping arc that took her well behind the sheep, where she crouched and stared at them, moving so slowly that they did not even realize she was herding them but walked gently, completely unstartled, towards the hurdles.

The wind was screaming through the trees, tearing at clothing, blowing up paper that lay flung carelessly on the field, and Pete was sure that the bitch could not hear a thing, but Sal was a veteran and she brought the four ewes through the hurdles, perfect outrun, perfect lift, Pete thought, and watched closely, noting every movement, admiring the slim graceful line of her as she worked, tail always aligned with her back, eyes never leaving the sheep.

The first drive after the return fetch took her little flock through the left hand hurdles, straight into the cross drive, through the right hand hurdles, and then, gently as summer breezes, into the shedding ring, where, before anyone had time to gasp, the shepherd had extended his crook and she had the first pair away, and the second pair were beyond the crook and the crowd were clapping.

'Seven minutes,' Pete said. 'Bet will never beat that.'

Bet wagged her tail, completely absorbed, watching as the other bitch herded the sheep to the pen, and came back to her master, standing on hind legs, paws on his shoulders, to receive his fervent praise. Contented, she dropped decorously beside him and walked off as if well aware that the thunder of applause was for her.

None of the dogs could beat Sal. Sam, trying his hardest, entered only for the third time, completed the course in eleven minutes, having the worst four sheep in the flock.

'Picked four clowns for your Dad,' Sal's owner said, standing beside Johnny, Sal relaxed at his feet, watching her successors, and intriguing Rex, who sat beside her with a proprietorial air. The four sheep were bold, brass-brazen, not caring about dogs. One of them turned to glare at Sam, who cowed her quickly, but another, feather-brained and foolish, only just old enough to stop being called a lamb, began to bounce, all four legs together, jumping like a rubber ball, higher and higher, refusing to leave the spot where she had started, entertaining the laughing crowd, so that Sam, his patience threadbare, barked at her in fury, startling her into a wild chase down the wrong side of the field before he could bring her back to pass through the first hurdles.

'That's bad luck,' the old man said. 'Sal couldn't have done so well if her sheep had behaved like that. Luck's at least half this game. Get bold sheep and the best dog is slowed down, and put out too, knowing he has a crowd watching. Not like working quietly on his own in his own time in the sheepfield.'

Pete came back, grinning wryly.

'Poor old Sam,' he said, and Sam jumped at him, tail wagging furiously, glad to be noticed.

By lunch time half the competitors had had their turns, and Sal was still in the lead. The men went off to the *Golden Crown* for lunch, a farmer's lunch of steak and kidney pudding and piled high mashed potatoes, and mounds of green cabbage, followed by apple pie and cream, the pastry golden crisp and crumbly so that Johnny, eating at a table with eight men, while his father enjoyed sheep talk and dog talk, fell into a trance, aware of nothing but the taste of food and the fact that he was out for the day for the first time in his short life, and had his father entirely to himself, without the older members of the family to interrupt. Ian was with Sue Wellans, and Tony for once in charge of the farm, taking care of everything in his father's absence, while Mum and Rosie were busy in the town buying wedding clothes, a thoroughly dull way to spend a day, Johnny thought. He hoped he would not have to go to Rosie's silly wedding, now only a few months away.

He ended his meal with bread and cheese, and, when his father's head was turned away, a sip of beer from the tankard of the white-moustached old man, Sal's owner, who was sitting beside him.

'Don't tell your Dad,' he whispered, with a wink. 'This'll make a man of you!'

Johnny sipped the beer and made a face. The old man laughed, caught the eye of the passing waitress and ordered fizzy lemonade, which came, to Johnny's delight, complete with a cherry on a stick. Small boys were rare in the dining-room of the *Golden Crown* and she was entertained by Johnny who was being as grown-up as he knew how.

The cheese board fascinated him. He could not choose at all, and in the end the man who carried it grinned and gave him a tiny square of everything and allowed him to dip the spoon in the Stilton. By the time the afternoon part of the trials began Johnny was so full he could scarcely move, and followed his father in a dazed dream in which he was grown up and entered the trials with Rex, and the dog completed the course in five minutes while the crowd cheered itself hoarse.

'Come on, Johnny,' his father said, as the child dragged behind him, 'Too much corn?'

Johnny came back to earth and grinned.

There were more cars and more people. The visitors were here now, as opposed to the morning crowd, which had been mainly farmers and shepherds. The town was out for a Saturday's enjoyment, and came with children and picnic gear, and worst of all, with dogs.

'Will all visitors please keep their dogs under control,' the loudspeaker blared on several occasions, but it was no use, for who wanted to spoil the day for Rollo or Rover or Fido, and a poodle chased the sheep when the farmer from Swallow's Hill had his dog half-way round the course, and a boxer engaged in a battle royal with Tom Ladyburn's dog ten minutes before Tom was due to start, and bit Lad on the leg, laming him so badly that running was painful, and the bite bled freely, and Tom retired, calling his dog in half-way, knowing he was finding the course too difficult with a bad leg.

Dai, treating the bite in the corner of the field, where his Land Rover did duty as an emergency First Aid Station, was irritable.

'Ought to ban all but sheep dogs from the field,' he said angrily, while Lad sat still and suffered stoically. 'This is the second bite I've dressed in twenty minutes.'

'Can't do without the gate money,' Tom said shrugging. 'It's no good turning folk away at five shillings a time for a car and one shilling for every occupant. Just have to put up with it.'

Bet completed her course well, coming down so fast during the return fetch that she finished in eight minutes, second now to Sal, and Pete came back whistling, to talk to Sal's owner about the finer points of dog training, and criticize the other entrants as their dogs worked.

Even Johnny, completely absorbed and anxious that no one should beat Bet's time and deprive his father of the five pounds that was the second prize, could see that the older men handled their dogs the best. Experience tells, his father always said, and he began to see, dimly, just what he meant.

'Young men don't have any patience,' Sal's owner said in disgust, as a stranger, who earned disapproval before he began, by appearing in creased grey flannels and a shapeless green jersey, sent his dog blind, right handed, against the crag, wasted two minutes in signals that the dog did not understand, and watched, grinning, as the sheep came pell-mell down the field, almost chasing into the crowd, and then turned and broke away, while neither dog nor shepherd seemed to know how to herd them back into a flock again.

After ten minutes had gone, the judge sent Sal and her owner to herd the sheep to the pen, and the young shepherd retired, still grinning, and called his dog, and drove off with a great revving of the engine of his small blue van.

Rex was next, and Johnny could hardly stand still. He watched as his father walked into the shedding ring, and sent Rex in a sweeping arc that brought him behind the four sheep. They watched him suspiciously, but Pete's whistle made the dog crouch, barely moving a muscle, and then, with infinite patience, he began to move and the sheep were away, scarcely knowing he had shifted them, in line, close together, through the hurdles and down to the ring.

Rex completed the first drive in record time, quicker even than Sal. He was unaware of the crowd, aware only of the sheep and his master's signals, striving to win approval, and knowing that Johnny would give it to him. He moved beautifully, winning himself murmurs of admiration from the shepherds, who saw at once that here was a born sheepdog, the skill of his ancestors making him outstanding.

'He'll beat Sal easily,' Sal's owner said, his eyes on his own watch, and on Rex, who had finished the cross drive and was bringing the sheep back to the shedding ring.

'He's going to win. He's going to win,' Johnny said, jumping up and down in his excitement, not noticing that a woman beside him was holding an Alsatian on a lead.

His foot came down on the Alsatian's paw, the dog snarled and turned and snapped at Johnny. Johnny cried out. A second later a bolting flash streaked down the field and took the Alsatian by the throat. Sal's owner caught Rex by the scruff, but the strange dog had attacked Johnny and deserved death, and it took five men to pull the collie off while Pete, disgraced, called to Bet to herd the sheep that Rex had deserted.

The birthday was ruined. Johnny was tearful, but knew that that would annoy his father even more. Rex had four bites, one of them a deep gash that tore across his head and through the outer edge of his ear, needing stitches, and the Alsatian looked as if it had been savaged by a wolf. The owner was furious until she discovered that the dog had bitten Johnny's thumb when he snapped at the boy. After that she dared say nothing, and Dai was acid as he tended her dog, telling her that only a fool would have brought such an animal to a sheep dog trials and she would be lucky if she wasn't sued, though he did not specify the reason, leaving her to feel guilt about Johnny's hand.

When Pete went to get Bet's prize money, the judge asked to see both Johnny and Rex, and Johnny went across to him reluctantly, aware of his bandaged hand, of his disgraceful dog, and afraid of a reprimand.

The old man looked down at the boy and smiled.

'He'll do very well when he's a year or so older,' he said. 'What happened? Did the Alsatian attack you?'

'I trod on his foot. I expect he got frightened and thought I did it on purpose,' Johnny said.

'Can't help accidents. You know, I wish I had a dog like yours. It doesn't often happen. But when it does ...'

Pete was consoled. The dog had only been defending the child, after all. And if Rex had not run down the field the Alsatian might have savaged Johnny. Dai had said it was completely untrained, a spoilt house pet, and not the right breed for spoiling.

Rex, in the short time he spent on the course, had made brilliant time. It was a pity that they did not know his pedigree. He might even win the International. But Pete had no time to spare to trace his dog's ancestry, even if he could. He looked down at Johnny, only partly consoled by the judge's words, his hand hurting, his dog labelled, as he had overheard, as unpredictable.

'What does unpredictable mean?' he asked his father, as they drove home through the reddening woods, and the dying sunlight that gilded the fells.

'You never know what will happen next.' Pete was relaxed and at ease, no longer angry with the dog.

'Someone said Rex was too unpredictable ever to be a winner,' Johnny said. Rex heard his name and thudded his tail, pushing his nose into Johnny's neck. Johnny put his arm round the dog. His dog. And suddenly he no longer cared whether Rex was unpredictable.

Pete did not answer. His eyes were on the road ahead, where traffic from the Show had slowed to a crawl. Only when the way was free again and he had turned into the quiet lane that led home, did he think about the comment.

The trouble was that the dog was too predictable. And that, no matter what happened, Johnny would always come first. He turned to say something of this to the boy, but Johnny was sound asleep, his head leaning against the seat, the dog's head on the child's shoulder, and Rex sat there guarding his treasure. Pete, seeing them wondered suddenly if the dog would attack him if he ever laid an angry hand on his small son.

CHAPTER SEVENTEEN

IT had been one of those days. Moira, suddenly urged to spring-clean, although it was not the season, had started at dawn by whitewashing the outbuildings attached to the house, and had then gone inside to make the kitchen spotless. The midday meal, of cold beef sandwiches with too much mustard, suited no one, and Johnny, in trouble at school, dawdled over his food, annoying his mother, and refused to hurry back, so that he was in more trouble for being late. He had refused to stay to school dinner.

Afternoon school was worse than morning. One of the Tanner boys picked a fight at playtime, and Johnny had a black eye to add to his woes. Mick Tanner had a bleeding nose, and lost a tooth that the teacher was sure had been already loose, although Mick insisted it was brand new, rock firm, a second tooth. Both boys were kept in for fighting, and Rex, waiting at the gate, drooping more and more as the time passed without sight of his small master, aggravated Moira beyond endurance.

She was sick of the dog, sick and tired of the way he and Johnny were all and everything to each other, no time for her nor anyone else. It was unnatural. This side idolatry, she thought, wondering where the tag came from. Johnny worshipped the dog, and it was bad for him, and bad for the dog.

Her back ached. The kitchen was spotless, but she was not, and no time for a bath, not with tea to make, and a meal for Ian and Pete when they came from tending the sheep.

Johnny would have to have eggs for his tea, but when she went to get them from the pantry, there were none. Tony had promised to collect them for her before he left for school.

As always he had forgotten. She went across to the hen-house with the basket, her feet dragging. If only she lived in a town, with no animals within earshot. No hens to feed, no pigswill to prepare, no eggs to collect.

No perpetual smell of sheep choking her nostrils, even though the air blew fresh and clean from the fells. If only there were houses close, and friendly people to pop in and out as they had in the town where she had been born.

No one to talk to. Rosie was hopeless, her mind on her wedding, now not so far off. Never listened to a word her mother had to say, nobody did, never cared if she were ill or well, so long as she washed their clothes, and cooked their food and cleaned up the mess they made.

If only she could get away. Right away, on her own, away from demands for clean shirts and where's my handkerchief, and the need to see that Johnny was decent for school; go off in torn jeans and his oldest jersey like the poorest village child if she didn't watch. And never a stroke of help from any of them, can't even collect the eggs for me, she thought savagely and picked one up so carelessly that it broke, making her clench her teeth and blink away tears of exhaustion.

Worked all day and all Pete would say was why bother, we don't mind a bit of mess. Makes it more like home, he'd say, not knowing that each speck of dirt goaded her, re-proached her, making her feel she could not even keep her house clean, making her feel useless, knowing as she did that she was no kind of wife for a farmer, not interested in the animals, afraid of and hating the dogs, unable to bear the constant talk of sheep and tractors, of car engines, and the prices at the lambing sales, and the price of wool.

She could pickle and bottle and cook as the other wives did, but without any pride, only doing it when it was necessary to store the summer surplus, and now Pete had promised her a deepfreeze if the next lambs made a big enough profit, and she felt he was doing it because she had failed him, failed to be a busy farmwife glorying in her rows of bottled fruit and pickles, entering for the summer shows and winning prizes with her cakes.

She had few friends in the village, feeling ill at ease with all of them, a stranger still, unable to join in their talk of cattle and of sheep, almost mantalk among many of them, they took so much part in the life of their men, having the pig money for their own, earning it too, by breeding their sows, and acting as midwife at farrowing time.

Birth on the farm revolted her, never getting used to the down-to-earth ways, brought up in a home where such things were not nice to mention, shocked to discover the life the men led out on the fells, often dragging the lambs from the ewes, and not squeamish about the talk afterwards, nor about coming home with blood on their hands, or bringing the orphans back for nursing.

She looked after the hens, though she detested them, so that she could feel entitled to the egg money, but three weeks of pig keeping had cured her for ever, and she could not handle the odd rank little sucklings that were brought to the outhouse, hating the smell of their wool and the sick sweet sour smell that seemed to envelop them, especially if they were upset by the cows' milk they were given.

Moira sat on the low wall in the sunshine, nursing the eggs, and watching Rex, wishing he would go away, wishing that she was the first creature that Johnny would greet, rushing to her, shouting 'Mum, Mum,' as he used to do when he was smaller and she was his whole world, his father only there in the evenings, almost a stranger to his son in his baby days.

None of them needed her. A housekeeper would do as well, and get better treatment. If only she could get away, right away, half-way over the world, maybe, have a holiday, the sort of holiday the magazines described, lazy days in the shining sun, a sun that brought heat and light, and not the soft glower that glimmered on the fells today. A place where the sea rolled warm and inviting up the sandy beaches and women in gay clothes lazed and cavalier courteous men laughed and talked, and idled, not up to their eyes from day-dawn to night-dark, down to earth in muck and mess and mire.

She looked out over the fells. She had been born where the trees were thick and green and leafy, and the summer full of bright blossom, and the downs golden under the warm light. The fells were bare and bleak and unwelcoming, the life on them harsh, often brutal, when death came in the guise of the questing fox or the sinuous weasel, snatching at duck or lamb or straying hen, leaving only the last traces and the feathers for her to find.

She hated the farm cats, with their frequent kills of mice and rats, often brought to her in triumph, making her sick. She disliked the half-wild kittens, finding no attraction at all in them, loathing the feel of fur beneath her fingers, feeling her back creep if one of them came into the house, an occurrence that was too frequent, for Johnny, given half a chance, would smuggle one up to bed with him, glorying in the tiny body, the warmth and soft responsiveness, and the rapturous wonder of its purr as he cuddled it close.

Life was bleaker than it had ever been. Moira contemplated a rapidly approaching old age, enslaved by the farm, and the needs of the animals, the children gone from home, and strange men to help, or perhaps Ian would bring a wife home, a strong girl who would glory in the work and she and Pete could retire, to a bungalow in a little town where the sea murmured on the beaches, and there was no wide vista of fell and mere and scree, but the comfort of frequent people and close-by houses, huddled for protection. But what would Pete do, away from the sheep?

Rex pricked his ears, and barked. Johnny was coming. Perhaps he would see her and smile at her, and forget the dog, but she knew the thought was futile. The gate rocked as the dog bounded against it, flinging himself at it as Johnny climbed the rails, never bothering to push it open. He jumped down, and the dog leaped at him, licking his face, yapping the welcome that was reserved only for Johnny. Moira watched them, and suddenly knew she was black jealous, and she hated the dog.

She stood up.

'Johnny, come and get your tea. The dog can wait,' she called, her voice sharp.

Johnny heard her, but he had had a terrible day. Being kept in was the last straw and he was a-burst with pent energy, needing to race and shout and scream and jump.

He pulled Rex's tail gently, an invitation for a game of tag. The dog jumped backwards, front legs outstretched, body sloped, and barked a challenge. Johnny flung himself at him, and Rex tore away, across the farmyard, behind the henhouse, with Johnny, laughing, in immediate pursuit.

'Johnny!' Moira called furious because she had been ignored and disobeyed.

The dog paused, and barked again. Johnny, taking a flying leap towards him, ready to roll and wrestle and play, missed his footing, and falling sideways, cannoned into his mother.

The basket of eggs fell to the ground, every one of them breaking. Johnny stood still, his face suddenly white, and Moira, enraged beyond all reason, slapped his face, again and again and again. Johnny looked up at her, his eyes desolate. He swallowed, saying nothing, and in that moment Rex raced towards them and stood in front of them, growling, barking, snapping at Moira, who was paralysed with slow horror.

'Rex!'

Pete's shout reached the dog, and stopped him. 'Down!' The voice had never been so angry. The dog dropped, hang-head, hang-tail. Moira stood shaking, the eggs at her feet slimy among the broken shells, tears of complete exhaustion creeping unnoticed down her cheeks. Johnny's face was marked where her hands had struck him, four fingers, plain as plain, reddening on each cheek.

'Bed!' Pete said to the dog, and Rex crept away, his tail between his legs; bent almost to the ground, while Johnny stood with his lips quivering, hating the world, and wanting to hurt his mother, to hit out at her, or kick her, because she could never understand.

'You'd better go to your room, too, Johnny,' Pete said, not knowing what to do, not knowing how the trouble had started, not understanding his wife, who stood as dumb as the dog, and stared at him, only her quick distressed breathing showing that she knew anyone was there.

Johnny went away, moving slowly, knowing he dared not defy his father, sure he was being wrongly punished. Everyone hated him. He had a hundred lines to write that night. It would take ages, sitting there writing over and over again,

I must not fight.

Mick Tanner had deserved it. Mick Tanner had said Johnny's Dad was a sheepstealer. Johnny conveniently forgot that he had said old Tanner was a good-for-nothing, poison-laying, no-good farmer, a phrase he had once heard Jasper use when talking to Ned.

As he went in through the door his mother spoke.

'That dog will have to be destroyed. He's dangerous. If you hadn't come he would have bitten me.'

Johnny did not wait to hear any more. He raced up to his room and flung himself on his bed, indulging in one of his rare tantrums, hitting the pillow with his fists, his face scarlet, choking his sobs, knowing that his father would be angry with him for showing temper.

Pete was too preoccupied to worry about Johnny. He put on the kettle and looked thoughtfully at his wife, conscious of her as a person for the first time for weeks. She never complained to him about herself, and though he knew she did not like farm life, he had never considered the subject. Make your bed, and lie on it, was his philosophy.

Passing the outbuildings, he had noticed the new white-wash, had seen the immaculate kitchen as he went into the house, and guessed at the reason for his wife's outburst. No one had ever smacked Johnny before. Both Pete and Moira believed that other forms of punishment were more suitable. Only a few weeks ago, when Johnny had thrown a ball through a window, he had been sent to walk three miles to the village shop for putty and glass, and had to help replace it, and also made to pay for the putty and a fraction of the cost of the window with his meagre weekly pennies. He had been much more careful since.

'You should have got Tony to do the outhouse,' Pete said, exasperated with her, making work for herself instead of letting things go a bit, and taking life easy now and then. Wouldn't take a day off and come to the sheepdog trials, wouldn't go and stay with her sister in Lancaster, saying she would only feel old and frumpy, Brenda being smart and go ahead, and married to a man with plenty of money. And how would the family manage?

'Tony can't even do the eggs, doesn't do a thing,' Moira said, the hot tea warming her, the chair soft to her tired back, sudden comfort from Pete's solicitude allaying the guilt she felt. She shouldn't have got so mad at Johnny. No wonder the dog went for her. Must have been crazy.

'Why didn't you tell me? I'll see to young Tony. It's daft to do it all. And the outhouses could have stayed a week or two, no need to have the place like a new pin. It only gets marred again.' Pete was bewildered. A good job he'd come home, or the dog might have bitten her. He'd come back for his wire cutters. One of the ewes had tangled herself in a length of wire some idiot had left lying in the grass. So twisted round her leg he couldn't free it without hurting her.

He poured himself tea.

'Johnny'll be hungry. He only had sandwiches for his lunch,' Moira said, struggling out of the chair, wishing she could sit for ever.

'Let Johnny wait awhile. He can eat with Ian and me. Be a change for him. He's getting quite big now. You sit down and rest a bit. You'll be laying yourself up before you know it, and where will we all be then?' Pete grinned at her affectionately, and she basked for a moment in rare peace, remembering why she had married him and tied herself to this upland farm, so alien to her own way of life.

It was pleasant without the children, without Johnny badgering and jumping around and asking questions, without Ian interrupting, talking about sheep or dogs. Pete began to tell his wife about his day on the fells, a thing he rarely did, talking about a hare that had run almost under his feet, half asleep it must have been, and wondering about a little boat he had seen sailing on Horton Mere. Both of them forgot about Moira's threat to Rex.

Johnny did not forget. He lay quiet, watching the leaves move on the tree outside his window. Rex was his and no one should touch him, and anyway, nobody loved Johnny. His mother hated him and hit him, his father didn't care and punished him when it wasn't his fault. He hadn't meant to bump into Mum and smash the daft eggs, and anyway the hens would lay some more eggs, what was all the fuss about? And of course Rex barked at people who went for Johnny. Stood to reason, Johnny thought, churlish with hunger.

Suppertime only added to his woes, for although he had meat and potatoes and carrots with the rest of them, instead of his own tea of eggs or baked beans, or a pie made for him alone, and bread and butter and scones and cake, he also had a lecture, and Pete, ignoring his rebellious expression, took the opportunity to try and make his small son less of a nuisance to his mother, and more helpful and thoughtful.

Johnny had been lectured all day. He said nothing, sat mutinous, glowering, and retired at last for the night, glad to be away from grown-ups who did nothing but go on and on. Couldn't fight. Couldn't play with a ball, or romp with the dog, it all made trouble for Mum.

Trouble at home, and trouble at school, he thought bleakly, switching off the light, knowing it was late, and he was very tired. He lay, looking at the ceiling, seeing moonlight pattern it with flecked leaf shapes, seeing it quiver and blend with the darkness and then shine again.

His mother came early to bed. He heard his father's voice across the landing.

'I'll be off to the *Swan* for a bit, and I'll do something about the dog in the morning.'

His mother's words came back to him. The dog will have to be destroyed. And quite suddenly he realized he had not done his lines. There would be more trouble at school. His dog dead, and himself at war, and no dog to come home to, no Rex to fly and meet him with licks and barks, no dog to chase and play with, ever again. As surely gone as Nell and Jasper, into a bleak other-world, where Johnny could not follow.

He sat and stared at the moonlight. It couldn't happen. It wasn't going to happen. He climbed out of bed and dressed, putting on his jeans and his thickest jersey, packing his school satchel with another jersey and his anorak. He opened his bedroom door. The house was still, only the ticking clock awake. He crept downstairs, into the kitchen, where he hastily raided the pantry, taking the end of a joint for Rex, and two pasties and a packet of biscuits for himself. He wasn't coming back, so he couldn't get into trouble.

He slipped out of the back door, closing it gently, and went to find Rex, taking collar and lead. The dog welcomed him eagerly, with fast moving tail. Johnny silenced him with a determined 'quiet' and Rex sat meekly, delighted by his unexpected bonus of a visit in the night.

Only the three cows, drowsing under the oak tree that sheltered their meadow, saw the pair slip stealthily over the wall, and vanish into the darkness.

CHAPTER EIGHTEEN

JOHNNY had never been alone in the moony dark. His heart thudded uncomfortably as he climbed through the dew-wet heather, and he was glad he had the dog for company. He climbed until he was above the house, on the high fells, the heather waist high about him, the bracken masking his view. He came to a bleak patch, where grey lichen-roughened rock let nothing else grow, and he looked down in wonderment at the sleeping village, the windows blind, all asleep save him, and Rex, and one other solitary dog that wailed a sonnet to the moon, longing for freedom from the chain that confined him.

Johnny sat on the rock with his arm round his dog, feeling the warm solid body comforting against him. Rex licked the boy's hand, unable to understand why they were here, alone, and at night, but willing to accept it, as he always accepted Johnny.

Behind them trees muffled the horizon, black against the brooding sky. High above them, the moon hung, and Johnny could see the old man's face, and could see, by its light, far over the fells, each tree clump a solid block hiding who knew what horrors. An owl hooted, long and mournful, and there was breathing close by in the dark, uncanny rasping breathing. Rex turned his head, but his nose told him it was only a fell pony, offering no danger, and a moment later, Johnny saw the pony shy away and heard the reassuring thump of its hooves as it cantered over the turf.

He would need to be a long way away by morning, or they would come and find him and take him home, and this time, if they caught him, there would be real punishment. If it had not been for the desolate feeling engendered by that knowledge, Johnny would have turned and run for the safety of his room, and the warm comfort of his familiar bed. Instead, he began to walk wearily, following a deer track that led through a tiny wood, where scary noises kept him walking at top speed, and out again on to the haunted moorland, where strange shapes moved beneath the moon, and a running sheep or fleeing cow or startled galloping pony made his heart stop, and his hand tighten on the dog's neck, holding on for reassurance.

High on the hills there was a lonely hut, where mist trapped shepherds might shelter. Johnny had been there twice with his father, and there he went, arriving at moonset, creeping into the deserted building, where he curled on the ground, the dog cuddled close for warmth. Rain drummed nightlong on the corrugated iron roof, but he was so tired that he slept until the sun rose high, and the fells were welcome with morning.

Rex was puzzled, but he watched over Johnny, greeted him fervently when he woke, and ate happily, gnawing at his meat while Johnny wolfed the pasties and ate biscuits, and longed for a drink. Water was his first concern, and soon found, in a small beck that chased enticingly over rock and rounded boulder, the banks guarded by bright heather. Both boy and dog were starved for water, and lay flat, side by side, revelling.

It was time to go, to go away, as far from home as possible, to climb the high fells to the big peak and slide and slip and slither down the other side. To walk along a lane, hungry again, feet dragging, and so dirty that even Johnny felt he needed a wash, to nod and smile at the passers-by, very few, but slightly curious, pretending to be a farm boy on an errand for his Dad, knowing that if they thought he was running away they would soon take him home again.

This was all strange territory, on the other side of the fells, in the opposite direction to his father's lands, and the familiar places where the home sheep grazed, and those in which the lambing flocks were sheltered. He had never been so far before.

By dinner time he could think of nothing but his huge

midday meal in the kitchen and his mother talking to him, listening to his questions, answering them. He was desperately hungry. His mouth began to water, his mind to think only of food. Of steak and kidney pie and rich brown gravy, of apple tart and cream, of crisp golden pastry, for frying bacon and egg, of cheese and fruit cake, and meals shared with Ned.

Perhaps if he went to Ned the old man would adopt him, and he need never go home. Ned would never kill Rex, no matter what he did. He hesitated, looking back wistfully over his shoulder, feeling very small under the wide-open frightening arch of the sky, but he knew that Ned would send him home, send him to school, tell him to go and learn, learn to be grown and a man. He didn't want to be grown, or a man. He didn't want to be like Ian, always off to see Sue Wellans, sometimes bringing Sue home with him, Sue who was so quiet and subdued and had not much to say for herself, walking with the little limp that had been left after the road accident, in which Jasper and Nell had been killed and Rex had saved Johnny's life.

They've all forgotten the nice things, Johnny thought. Only think of bad things, never good ones, like the times he dried up for Mum. Never did remember how he made his bed one day, and another day he chopped some wood, not much, the chopper was too big, and Dad had been cross, but he did do it. Only remembered the day he broke the ladder in the hayloft, and the day he started the tractor and it crashed into the barn.

Johnny sat down beside the road, and stared at nothing, full of self-pity. Rex, sensing his mood, put a sympathetic head on his knee, and gloomed with him.

A tractor passed, the lurching trailer filled with hay. The driver stopped to adjust his load, and then climbed back into the driving seat again, whistling, and nodded to Johnny.

'Want a lift?' he called, not much more than a lad himself, and sorry for the boy, huddled so forlornly by the roadside, no doubt sent on a long errand by his Mum, and tired.

Johnny and Rex jumped on to the trailer, and Johnny

held the dog tight, as they jolted over the rough muck-patched surface. He was dazed with hunger, and feeling sick. They stopped at a farm gate.

'This is as far as we go,' the driver called out cheerfully. 'Helped you on your way?'

'Yes, thanks,' Johnny said, and trudged off, his feet dragging.

The road was busy. Passing cars bothered him, so that he soon turned back and climbed the fells, wondering if he could find an isolated farmhouse, and pretend he was lost, or not pretend, he was now thoroughly lost, and beg a meal. Rex, stopping to sniff at the scent of rabbit, pulled on his lead, whining.

They were on a bridle path, climbing steadily. On either side of them were pine woods, and here the foresters were working. Johnny glimpsed the men, avoiding them. One had left food in his saddle bag. The dog sniffed at it and whimpered, and looked at Johnny, and Johnny looked at it longingly. If only he dared. But instead he trudged on, swallowing the saliva that flooded his mouth.

The ground was slippery after the night's rain. Both boy and dog were starving, and had it not been for the thought that he was now in dire trouble, and Rex would be shot when he got home, too dangerous to keep, Johnny would have gone to the foresters and confessed his plight. As it was, he kept walking, hoping that some solution would come to him. Perhaps an old shepherd, high on the moors, would give him food and ask no questions. Perhaps he could find an old woman who wanted a boy and a dog for company and would keep him for ever. Perhaps he could get to the sea and stow away in some ship with Rex, and find a home in another country.

There was no lack of ideas. Johnny had too much imagination for his own good at the best of times. It led him to devise all kinds of mischief, both at home and at school, just as it had led him to run away, and, now, to keep walking. He did not even stop to consider that his parents might miss him and search for him. He was sure they would be only too glad to be rid of him, not to have to clean up after him or pay for the things he broke.

It was always the same.

'Johnny! You cost me a small fortune. That's the third thing you've broken this week.'

'Johnny. I don't know what we're going to do with you. Haven't you any sense?'

And then she smacked me just for breaking her silly old eggs, Johnny thought, needing to goad himself, so that anger kept him walking. He wanted to sit down and give up, he was close to despair, he had never been so hungry in all his short life.

The smell of stewing meat was elixir. The dog sniffed, and began to pull at his lead, and Johnny, catching the delight that scented the wind, followed him, swallowing frantically, not caring who or what had food up there on the empty fells, only knowing that he must eat, and quickly.

Old Sam saw the boy and the dog coming. It did not surprise him. Nothing surprised him, living as he did in an oddly simple half-world that he seldom understood, having been given as his heritage the mind of a rather unworldly and sinful saint, so that he accepted life with astonished childlike pleasure, and took Johnny's company as a gift from his own personal deity, with whom he was on close and friendly speaking terms.

He had built a small fire, knowing how to bank it carefully, how to make it on rock, so that it would not spread and catch the heather. Over it, in an old biscuit tin perched across two rocks, he was cooking a rabbit that he had caught that morning, together with a handful of onions and turnips and potatoes, and carefully hoarded herbs, which were good for keeping away rheumatism and winter ills, and the coughs that often plagued him.

Johnny looked at the old man, seeing shrewd blue eyes hidden in a mat of grey hair, grizzled beard meeting flowing locks, a long tattered overcoat, kept together with large safety pins, a bright tartan scarf, given him by a woman who heard him cough, and was shocked by the noise of his groaning lungs, and shabby old battered boots that would have disgraced a guy on Bonfire Night.

'I'm lost,' Johnny said, aware that he should not talk to

strangers, yet suddenly anxious for companionship, no matter what kind.

'And hungry,' Old Sam said. He smiled at the boy. 'It's nice to have company. I got a spare plate.'

He brought it out, wiped it on the grass, and filled it with stew, giving Johnny a battered spoon which he first cleaned on a bracken leaf. He fished two large pieces of meat out of the tin for the dog.

'Too hot for you, as yet, feller,' he said. 'That dog won't bite?'

'Only if you try and touch me,' Johnny said, suddenly aware that he had a guardian with him and that no one could harm him so long as Rex was alive. 'He's a good dog if I tell him to be.'

Rex wagged his tail. His eyes watched every movement of the spoon from plate to mouth, and he looked at the pieces of meat on the grass, drooling in agonized impatience until Sam decided they were cool enough and threw them to him. He attacked them greedily, worrying at the meat, desperate for food.

'Where you from?' Old Sam asked, between noisy mouthfuls.

'Over near Bruton,' Johnny answered, his mouth crammed tight, the food warming him, making him strong again, determined not to go back and have his dog killed because it was dangerous.

'You go down the path and into the village and find the policeman and he'll see you safe home,' Sam said.

Johnny, warm again, and no longer famished, was unwilling to consider home.

'This is very good rabbit,' he said appreciatively, changing the subject deftly.

'Come by it honest,' Sam said hastily. 'There's a farmer, see. Lets me snare on his land and sleep in his barn when it's wet. I likes it up here when it's dry. I can do jobs for him, like. Getting the eggs in, and such, he comes to rely on me, does old Nat Thomas.'

'Not that I don't think it's wrong to lay claim to animals for your own, just because they happens to be on your land,' Sam added, wondering if even Johnny would swallow this flight of pure fancy, a kind of dream fulfilment, of being trusted and honoured, instead of always despised, old Sam good-for-nothing, could he help it if the wandering was in him, and no urge ever to settle in one place, tie himself to dull everyday dreariness, and not the money to pay for his whims, like some folk had?

'Animals,' he explained to Johnny, 'was made after God made the world. And then He put us in, to feed off the animals. And then the Devil come along, and he invented money. And because of the Devil, them 'as got no money don't eat, unless they're clever. Got to be clever. But God never meant for all them farmers to lay claim to rabbits as live on their land. What rabbit ever stayed on one spot? Might go off and feed across a road, or next door garden, and whose rabbit is it then?'

Johnny was not sure that he cared. The rabbit felt extremely good in its present site, and his conscience was perfectly clear. He liked Old Sam and thought he was funny. He was particularly intrigued by the way the old man hissed his s's, spitting the words out through the gaps in his teeth, the last remaining yellow tumps like the teeth of a very old horse.

Sam enchanted him further by rolling his tobacco and chewing it.

'Broke me last pipe, and it's as good as any other way,' he explained to Johnny.

Johnny was sleepy. Rex, full fed, drowsed with his nose on Johnny's leg, his ears wakeful, ready to spring to action if need be. Sam sniffed the air, and looked uneasily about him, as sensitive to wind and weather as any wild animal.

He could not decide what was troubling him. Johnny was almost asleep, leaning against his dog, and the old tramp decided to let the boy rest a while longer, and then persuade him to go down and find someone to look after him and take him home. Sam felt that trouble might be brewing if he kept the child with him. He had never been in trouble. A warning for poaching, but that was all. He was careful not to steal, although he often begged. He had a healthy respect for the law, and desired to keep his own freedom. But he could never see that wild birds and beasts could belong to any one man.

Once he had tried living in a home for old men. The memory of it returned to him, and he wrinkled his nose, remembering the sour old man smell, the fustiness, the enclosed walls, and the terrifying nights when other men had been too close to him, snoring and snuffling and choking and sniffing, crowding in on him, stifling him, until he had left and come away to live again free, as his own private God had intended. It was the Devil who made cities, not the Lord, Sam thought.

He looked down now at the world that he loved so much that he preferred living poor and free so that he could inhabit it. Below him the path lay broad and wide, joined by a fork just beyond the lake that imaged the sky. A small wind ruffled the silken surface, and the sound of wind in the trees beside him, of water licking gently at the grassy shore, of a lark calling, high above him, was all the music he wanted.

The lake narrowed, thrust out a watery finger that vanished under a humped stone bridge, and beyond the bridge, small as a toy, and at this distance as neat and trim and tidy, was a sprawling stone farmhouse, its sides flanked by towering barns, the whitewashed cowsheds bright against the sky, hidden at the rear under brooding dark trees that clumped together to shelter the buildings from the prevailing wind that tore down the rocky gully behind them. Sam looked up the farther hill, at the stony crack in which bushes clung and huddled, and far away, over the strangely sulphur tinted fells, to the horizon. He sighed, savouring every sight and sound, holding it to him, as aware as any artist of the beauty of the landscape, and the private peace of the bare bleak places where he loved to tramp.

It was time for the boy to go. He moved his hand, intending to shake Johnny, and at once Rex was awake, his teeth bared in a silent snarl, defying the man.

'Hey, sonny.' Sam spoke sharply and Johnny woke and blinked and rubbed his eyes, startled to find himself on the open fells and not at home in bed.

'Look.' Sam pointed. 'See that farm? They've got a telephone. You go down there, and tell them who you are and they'll find your folks for you. Not right for a little boy like you to be wandering alone. And don't you go speaking to any strangers,' Sam added, neither he nor Johnny seeing any incongruity. 'Never know where you are with folk, and they're not all decent like you and me.'

Johnny stood up and sighed. He was so tired. He set off down the hill, with Rex beside him, and Sam watched them go, and then, muttering to himself, put plates and mugs and cutlery into his old sack, stamped out his fire, and set off himself, making for the other side of Coniston, where there was a friendly smallholder who would give him a meal and a bit of tobacco.

Before he had gone far he sniffed again, and this time he knew what was troubling him. It was the smell of snow. The sombre sky should have warned him. Already treacherous flakes were gliding down to cover the peaks. It did not matter to him. He had weathered too many years to care. He would sit with his back against a tree or a rock and his tattered coat pulled round him, and endure discomfort stoically, as he endured everything else, rain, gale, and mist, always finding a place to bide, or a mite of shelter. But the boy was different. There was danger for him in a blizzard. And he might wander, and there were boggy places on the fell, and sheer drops where the child might find disaster.

'Hey, sonny, sonny,' he called, stumbling back to Johnny in a shambling run. But Johnny was too far away and the words drifted on the air, and the white snow came in blown flakes, swirling on the wind and blotting out the land, and Johnny and the dog were isolated in silence, and nothing else lived in the wild white world but the two of them, bewildered and blinded by the soft clinging flakes.

CHAPTER NINETEEN

No one missed Johnny, that first night. Moira, exhausted, went to sleep early. She rarely went in to see her small son as he slept too lightly and if he woke during the evening, seldom settled until late, and in his waking time anything might happen, from an overturned bookcase as he tried to swing from bed to chair without touching the ground, to a broken window, as he tried to lob his ball through the open part at the top, without touching the glass.

Pete, after his wife had gone to bed, went down to the *Swan*.

'Snow coming. Got the sheep on low ground?' Ned asked, as the farmer swung through the door.

'Snow? Rubbish!' Pete said. It was early November, and as yet quite warm.

'Rain tonight. Snow tomorrow night. I'm telling you,' Ned said. 'Seen weather like this before. Catches everybody out.'

'I'll bring them down in the morning then,' Pete said, laughing. 'Can't do much harm. I'll believe you. Thousands wouldn't.'

'You'll see.' Ned drowned his small mouth in bitter, and blew the froth at his dog. 'I'm dry tonight.'

'And you gave me a tip off, you old scrounger. Give Ned another, Mrs. Jones.' Pete took his own drink, paying for it with small change which he counted carefully.

'You look glum,' Ned said, always observant.

'Moira lost her temper and slapped Johnny and Rex went for her. I said we'd have to put the dog down. Can't keep him if he's going to go for anyone that lays a hand on the kid. It's not safe. And dear knows what Johnny will do. He lives for that dog.'

'Dog can be cured,' Ned said irritably, wondering if everyone in the world but he were daft. 'Only take a few days, and you and I and Johnny can soon put him straight. No need to get rid of the dog.'

'Anyone'd think it was your dog,' Pete answered crossly. The dog seemed to cause nothing but problems. 'How would you cure him?'

'The way I cured that boxer of the doctor's from sheep-worrying,' Ned said promptly. 'Or on the same lines. You ought to remember. Cured him with your ram.'

Pete did remember. The boxer, a valuable dog, had had three goes at his sheep, and Ned showed him a trick that the older shepherds had used, putting the boxer in to chase a ram. The ram had the better of that game, and after being butted sideways, endways, and tail over head, the boxer had decided he was afraid of sheep and given no trouble since.

'Can't use a ram to cure him,' Pete said.

Ned made an impatient explosive sound between closed lips that set the dogs barking and the other men looking at him.

'Bring Johnny and the dog to me, and I'll go for Johnny. If the dog goes for me you can shake him. He won't try more than three times, I'll bet you. He's a bright dog and he'll soon get your meaning.' Ned glared at Pete defiantly. Put the dog down without even trying to break a habit. What had got into him?

Although he did not entirely realize it, guilt had got into Pete, guilt because Moira was overwhelmed and overworked and he had not even noticed. And Johnny was a handful, no doubt of that, and she not nearly as young as she'd been when the others were small. And Rex had been a problem, almost from the start. Pete resented the dog's attachment to Johnny, so that he could never be used for herding after school had ended, having to go home and meet the boy. Yet, in all fairness, the dog had been given to Johnny, and he had no right to complain.

At home, he was greeted by an anguished bellow. He went into the cow byre, and found Ian standing beside Tara, who was due to calve.

'Going to need the ropes, Dad,' Ian said, thankful that his father had come at last.

Pete went to the cow and soothed her, examining her carefully.

'Going to need Dai,' he said at last. 'Go and phone him, and then come back here. No sleep for any of us tonight.'

Dai, arriving as rain began to sluice down, took command, but it was milking time before Tara's calf was safely delivered. Tara herself, exhausted and weak, showed signs of fever.

The three of them, sitting in the kitchen, drinking strong coffee to wake them, had no strength left for words. Pete nodded to Rosie when she came downstairs.

'Cow all right?' she asked, filling the kettle again.

'Not so good, but she'll recover. Better get home or I'll never get through the day's work. Got an operation on a dog this morning. No end to it.' Dai yawned, nodded, and trudged away. Pete watched the Land Rover drive out of the yard, mesmerized.

'Pete!' Moira's voice, from the landing, was sharp with anxiety. 'Johnny's not in his room.'

'That's not unusual,' Pete said, not surprised. 'He'll be around, somewhere.'

'He's taken his spare jersey and his anorak, and the dog's collar and lead.' Moira came downstairs and went to the pantry, as she spoke, knowing she had to prepare food for the menfolk so that they could get out to the sheep. 'And two pasties and the end of my meat,' she added, on a rising note of dismay.

'I'll go and look for him,' Ian said. He took his jacket and went into the yard, finding Rex gone, as he had known he would, and no sign of Johnny in byre or stable, or behind the haystacks, or in the loft above the old barn.

'Johnny. Johnny!'

The calls resounded, but there was not a movement, not a stir in answer, and Moira sat on the edge of the old kitchen chair, her face white.

'He must have heard us talking about the dog and run away,' she said.

'He won't be far,' Pete said, reassuringly.

'You don't know Johnny. When his mind is made up ...
He might have asked for a lift in a lorry. He might have hurt
himself ... We don't know how long he's been gone.' And
it's all my fault, she thought miserably, knowing she put
stress on the wrong things, and had no time for the child.
Sure that this had been sent to punish her, taking all the
guilt of womanhood on her own shoulders, blaming herself for everything that went wrong, even to the cow's awkward calving, too worried and bothered to sort out her
feelings.

By lunchtime half the village were looking for Johnny,
Ned up on the fells, calling till his throat was raw, Fleck beside him, hunting rabbits gaily and absurdly, annoying his
master who felt there should be some trace of the child, some
sign that Johnny had come this way, some clue to his passing.
But the rain had washed every trace away.

The Huntsman, taking his own hound, Ranger, climbed
the lambing slopes up to the fells, where he could see for
miles, using a borrowed spyglass. Only the sheep and a stray
fell pony, and a sparrow hawk hunting, revealed themselves
to his questing gaze.

Pete and Ian took turns to walk over moor and bogland,
and Ian scoured the quarry, while Pete went to the huts that
he used himself when benighted on the fells. With each hour
their spirits sank lower, and at two that afternoon, Pete
went to Ben Timmins, who listened frowning.

'Should have come before,' he said, ringing through to
the town, asking for dog handlers, and a search party. 'Even
if it's a false alarm. It's better than coming too late. When
did Johnny go off?'

But Pete did not know. It might have been any time during the night, or even the evening before. None of them had
thought to check and see if the child was there. Why should
they? Johnny had never done such a thing before.

Nor had he had need, Pete thought, remembering that
Johnny thought his dog was to be killed. Damn that dog, of
course it could be cured of what was only a natural habit.
Dogs were cured of worse faults than that. Needed time
and patience, that was all. And Moira's consent. And that
might be more difficult.

By nightfall all the men in the village were out. They all knew Johnny. The boy and his dog were a familiar village sight, amusing all of them, and Johnny, never self-conscious or shy, was known to every one of them, helping this one with haying, and that one with egg collecting, visiting Bess for her cookies and Mrs. Jones for orange squash on hot days home from school, knowing that wherever he went he was welcome.

At home, Moira, for the first time, found herself a part of the village, and not a looker-on, for most of the women dropped by with a word of comfort for her, and brought small gifts as a token of their concern, a pot of jam, or a jar of red cabbage, being able to say with gifts the sentiments that were too awkward to put into words.

Bess, toiling up the hill, her rheumatism now a permanent penance, brought a basket of apples from her big cooking-apple tree, and sat in the warm kitchen, at a loss for words, her mind on the small boy out on the fells, and the weather changing and cold, and snow coming, as she'd heard on the news.

When the police dogs arrived, Ian took Sam and Bet and began to move the sheep to lower ground, irritated by the woolly, bleating animals that prevented him from joining the search. Johnny was a little devil, he thought wryly, sending Sam to gather a stray ewe determined not to be parted from her favourite place. It was blowing up cold. It was not pleasant to think of Johnny out there, God knew where, by himself, and over twenty hours now. He might be anywhere, lying in one of the hidden gullies, or buried deep in a bog, or miles from here, on a lorry. One thing, no one could hurt him so long as Rex was alive.

Ian watched the woolly backs massing the lane. Sam kept them trotting along, and Bet herded the stragglers, both working together without need for commands, which was as well, as Ian was distracted. Never before had the stretch of the fells and the bleak hills seemed so remote, so vast, and so lonely. And if snow came . . . Ian thought of the many bodies of sheep he had moved each year, after the last snow had gone. And a small boy was not as hardy as a sheep. He began to feel sick.

Ben Timmins called hourly at Five Ways to see if Johnny had returned. His query and Moira's headshake, and his own lack of news became part of a deadly routine, as he cycled away to contact the squad car that was parked beside the bridle path leading on to the fells. The rain had done its work thoroughly. The dogs could not pick up a trace of scent anywhere.

By nightfall more police were drafted into the area. They were strung out along the slopes, each man hunting as carefully as any hound on a trail, but this trail was stone cold. Reporters drove up in cars, and tried to see Moira, but Ian kept them away, becoming surlier as the hours went by, ready to pick a fight, simply to relieve his feelings. Moira and Rosie sat and drank cup after cup of tea, scarcely aware that they were doing so, and made awkward small talk when other women came by to see them, knowing it was kindness and not curiosity that brought them to visit.

By nightfall Johnny was news, a small piece of news in a television newsreel, a bigger sensation on the front page of the evening papers, pictures of the police strung out over the heather, of the dogs nosing the ground, of the farmhouse where Johnny lived. Some to be reproduced, and others to be filed, ready for use if there should prove to be a final disaster.

Those reporters who heard the tale of the dog that always met Johnny from school had a story after their own hearts. The boy with the dog was just the thing to appeal to the readers, and by morning Johnny was much bigger news, for he was still missing, and the fells were masked with snow, deep drifting snow that made it difficult for men and dogs, and there was more to come.

Moira, unable to eat or drink, sat watching the white flakes falling, remembering other winters, other blizzards, and she hated the fells and the farm and the sheep. If she had married a townsman, Johnny could not have been lost, out in that wicked white wilderness where sheep lay in the drifts for weeks and men could flounder and die and be found months later when the snow cleared. There had been a shepherd, only last year. . . .

Pete, standing beside the squad car, listening to the

messages that came in, drinking tea laced with brandy that one of the farm wives had provided, too numb to notice who had given it to him, for the first time in his life hated and feared the fells. He too remembered sheep. And a dog that had fallen into a snow drift. And that shepherd, only last year . . .

He turned as a big policeman, burly in his dark uniform, an eager Alsatian beside him, came hurriedly down the slope, black against the snow. The light was faint now, cloud over the moon and more snow in the cloud, which hung low, deadening the world beneath it.

Pete looked up. The policeman shook his head, pity tightening his throat. He had a son, just Johnny's age.

Pete turned and trudged up the hill, glancing at the sheep, safe in their winter field; even if snow lay thick they would not be covered, and he would bring them food.

At that moment he hated them. He hated the farm, and hated the fells. He went into the byre, and gave Tara a drench.

If only Johnny was safe . . .

But there was little hope, now.

CHAPTER TWENTY

JOHNNY knew about snow. Only eight months before they had been marooned for five days, unable to get to the village, or up on to the tops, cut off by a sudden unseasonable late blizzard that caught the new lambs and the weak ewes. Snow could kill.

Rex, keeping close to Johnny, stopped frequently to paw the wet flakes away from his eyes. The two of them went on, snowboy and snowdog, plunging down towards the house that they had seen below them, and that offered shelter. They must get out of the snow, out of the drifting danger that could hide and freeze and smother.

The ground was rapidly masked with a smooth deceptive cover. Johnny did not see the small boulder that rolled beneath his foot, throwing him against another, larger, outcrop of craggy rock. He fell, and lay still, dropping the dog's lead.

Rex nosed him. Johnny did not move. The collie pawed him, barking, anxious, and then the dog whimpered, nosing the boy's face, until he caught the tang of blood from a deep cut that slashed across the child's forehead.

Rex barked again. His paw pulled at the boy, commanding him to wake, to jump up, to run, away from the danger of this deep drifting uncanny stuff that made life so uncomfortable. Puzzled, the dog sat down, but the snow worried him, and the boy worried him, and at last he decided to look for men, men who could help.

Twice he ran towards the farmhouse, now immediately below them, close enough to hear the sound of voices, and of churns being moved across the yard. Twice he came back, trying to rouse the boy, anxious to see him stand and run and jump.

At last he gave up and ran down the fellside, picking his way over the easiest ground, impatient of the lead that dragged behind him, speeding as fast as he could towards the sounds of movement from below.

The farmer at Seven Birches had his mind on the weather, on the need to finish milking, on the possibility of being snowed up in the morning and unable to get the milk away. He was startled by the dog that came bounding at him out of the dusk, lead trailing, barking vigorously.

'Where did that dog come from?' he yelled across the yard, to the cowman, who was herding the cattle back into the field, his own dog busy.

'Shepherd on the fells?' the cowman asked.

'With a lead? Like as not someone in trouble up there The dog wants us to follow him. Look at him.'

Rex was moving towards the wall, looking over his shoulder, returning to bark, and running off again, desperate to attract attention, to make them go with him, to fetch Johnny and bring him out of the weather and into the warm.

The farmer went for brandy, and a warm coat. The cowman shut the cattle into the field, blew on his hands, and turned his back on the many jobs waiting in the milking parlour. Human needs came first, and anyone lying up there on a night like this . . . He shuddered.

Rex ran in front, guiding them through the dusk. Johnny was lying where he had fallen, but he was conscious again, and sick with the pain in his twisted ankle and the thumping ache in his head, and frightened by the snow and the fact that Rex had left him alone, wondering where the dog had gone, and if the dog had been hurt too and was lying somewhere out of sight and sound.

He tried to sit up when he heard Rex bark.

'Rex!' he called.

His voice floated thinly over the fells.

'Good God. It's a child,' the farmer said, and began to run, anxious that the child should not move, for he lay near a small gully, and there snow always drifted thick and deep.

Johnny looked up at the man who stooped over him.

'I'm lost,' he said, into a mist of sickness and pain, and

was glad to have a shoulder to cuddle against, the warm re-assurance of the farmer's thick duffle coat, the sound of the man's voice, talking to comfort him, telling him how the dog had come and fetched help, and so prevented him from dying out there on the snowy fells.

'They want to shoot my dog. He went for Mum when she smacked me,' Johnny said forlornly, and the pent tears of the past days suddenly spilled over, and he was small and cold and tired and defenceless and soon he would be with-out his dog. Rex, walking beside them, licked his small master's hand, and made matters a thousand times worse, so that the farmer was glad to hand over the dirty and sob-bing bundle that he carried to the capable hands of his wife, who, being a grandmother ten times over, knew exactly what to do.

The telephone bell was no longer a welcome sound in the farmhouse at Five Ways. They were all in the kitchen when it rang. Moira was exhausted by waiting, unable to feel warm, unable to feel anything except a numb terror for Johnny, out there in the dark, with the snow piling up, creeping over him, cutting him off from home and safety.

Tony was for once more concerned with family affairs than with his own life, as captain of the school Rugby First Fifteen, cricket captain, leader always in the debating society, school vice-captain, house captain, busy and im-portant, never at home, wanting to be a vet, yet not bother-ing with the animals. He was standing by the telephone, drinking soup from a mug, warming his hands after a long futile search beyond Bruton.

Rosie was knitting, her needles racing, anything to dis-tract her mind. She wanted to cry for Johnny, but knew that if she did, her mother would cry too and her father be furious, and besides, there were strangers there. The Hunts-man, and Ranger lying on the kitchen floor, and Ned with Fleck, and Bet and Sam had crept in too, unnoticed, and were beneath the table, as the other dogs were inside, and no one had remembered them.

Sue Wellans had come with an apple pie that her mother had made, and was now cooking, aware that Moira had no heart left for mundane things. Ian had gone out again, desperate with impatience, and was combing the fells near the quarry.

Ben Timmins had called with yet another negative report. His face was grey with weariness. He had been out all night, and his exhausted mind worked over the more unpleasant possibilities, the dog shot by a crank, the child killed by some lunatic up there on the fells. Surely the dogs would have found a trace, at least. He had not been to bed for thirty-six hours.

The ringing phone was meaningless. Another negative report from the squad car, who kept in touch with the searchers on the fells by walkie-talkie, and rang back at intervals, from a call box, to see if Johnny had come home by himself.

It was Rosie who, at last, nerved herself to answer it, her face set. They watched her, so tired that they were incurious, expecting nothing, or at most bad news. She put down the phone on the table, turned to them, and stared blankly at them, unable to speak for the sudden tears that poured down her cheeks.

'Rosie!' Tony looked at her in horror.

'He's safe, Johnny's safe,' she sobbed and ran out of the room and up the stairs to find privacy, leaving Pete to stride across the floor and answer the farmer at Seven Birches. He had guessed that his news might prove overwhelming, having heard Johnny's story by now.

Moira began to shake. She could not stop. No part of her seemed under control, and it was Sue who helped her to bed, who filled hot water bottles, and who sat beside her, talking about anything and nothing, remembering her own black days after Jimmy and Jasper had died, and the more understanding because of them.

There was jubilation on the fells, as the news came over the walkie-talkie sets. Shoulders were unconsciously thrown back, the men grinned and laughed and chatted, calling to one another, playing with the dogs. One of the policemen hid himself. The dogs could not go away without a find, or they would be discouraged, and not seek so well next time. But this was a game, a piece of foolery, and the sound of wisecracks and relieved voices drifted down the fells.

The snow had stopped falling, the cloud cleared, the moon hung low in the sky, glowing on a land that was masked and blanketed, its folds and gullies, its rocks and trees and heather patches, its whole day-by-day identity smoothed, glistening faintly, landmarks gone, the fells new-born, unfamiliar, hiding themselves under a cover that lent them an elfin splendour, and an air of mystery.

The squad car took Pete through the night to Seven Birches. He had no thought in his head but that Johnny was safe. He had almost forgotten the dog. The child was hurt, but not badly. A sprained ankle, the doctor said, a cut that had needed two stitches and slight concussion. A week in bed, and he would be as good as new again.

Johnny was waiting, dressed in a pair of flowered pyjamas that were much too big for him, and wrapped in two blankets. Rex lay beside him.

'Rex saved me,' Johnny shouted as soon as his father came into the big kitchen, where the patterned plates shone on the old dresser and a huge log-fire lent warmth and life to the stone-flagged room that was the centre of the farm house, the parlour never used except for weddings, christenings and funerals.

'Rex came and found Mr. Peters and barked and Mr. Peters followed him and they found me and I didn't get snowed up because Rex saved me. You won't shoot him now, will you?' He ended, his voice desperate, pulling away from his father, who had tried to take him in his arms.

'We'll never shoot Rex,' Pete promised, knowing that from now on such an action was unthinkable. 'And I think he'd better be your dog all the time and only come out with the sheep when he wants to. He's a one-man dog, Johnny, and you're his man.'

Johnny's face relaxed. His hand went down to the dog, and the dog licked it, tail wagging so hard that it thudded a drum roll on the floor.

The Peters waved as the car drove off. Johnny, cuddled against his father, his world secure again, slept the whole way home, and the dog lay beside him, his head on the boy's legs, his eyes never leaving Johnny's face. Once home, he went, as if by right, to the rug by Johnny's bed, and Moira, finding him when she ran in to see her small son, only shook her head, knowing that she had lost for ever, and also knowing that the dog had saved the child's life, and that she could never feel hatred towards him again.

Two days later, sitting in the *Swan*, reporting Johnny's recovery, lightheaded with relief, Pete grinned across the table at Ned. Ned was partly concerned with dipping his fingers in his beer for Fleck to lick, but he caught Pete's glance.

'What's up then?' he asked.

'Remember that bet? That you'd find me a dog I couldn't train to the sheep?'

Ned grinned, and waited.

'I think you've won it. Rex has me beat. He's Johnny's dog, and I'll never make him into a sheepdog, putting the sheep before everything else. Not even going to try.'

He took a folded five-pound note from his pocket and tossed it over to Ned, who caught it as it slid on the table, opened it, admired it, tucked it away, and then brought it out again.

'I'm rich,' he said, laughing. 'Drinks all round on me, Mrs. Jones!'

The men turned to him, roaring with laughter, for here was Ned in the money at last, Ned who never had a penny to spare and was always thankful for a free drink, here he was repaying his debts.

'Here's to Rex, the dog that Pete couldn't train!' Ned said, grinning, holding his beer mug high. Fleck begged, the men laughed again, the dogs barked at the sound, and Mrs. Jones, taking a rare drop herself, looked on with satisfaction as the rafters of the *Swan* echoed the noise.

In the farmhouse, Moira looked in to say goodnight to Johnny. Johnny was asleep. Beside him was the old basket chair, turned towards the bed, and there Rex lay, the boy's hand buried in the thick handsome ruff that protected the collie's neck. The dog opened one eye and looked at her warily.

'You old rogue,' she said, and laughed, and for the first time in his life he wagged his tail for her, and went back to

174

sleep, his place now firmly established in the farmhouse. She went out of the door. Things would never be the same again. When Johnny plagued her she'd look back on the past days and remember, and be thankful he was there to play the goat about the place.

The moonlight, slipping between the curtains, shed an errant beam across the boy's dark head, and silvered the dog. Rex woke, instantly alert, lest there be danger. But all was safe, and he curled himself again, this time lying with his head on Johnny's shoulder. The boy moved his arm, encircling the dog sleepily, wakened, and looked at the snow-covered sweep of the fells, gleaming beyond his window.

'Rex!' he whispered, knowing his world was safe again.

Rex beat a triumphant tantara with his tail, and then fell asleep. Boy and dog shared a mutual dream in which the fells were white with Johnny's sheep and the dog herded them, and day and night they were never parted.

A SELECTED LIST
OF CORGI BOOKS

WHILE EVERY EFFORT IS MADE TO KEEP PRICES LOW, IT IS
SOMETIMES NECESSARY TO INCREASE PRICES AT SHORT NOTICE.
CORGI BOOKS RESERVE THE RIGHT TO SHOW AND CHARGE NEW
RETAIL PRICES ON COVERS WHICH MAY DIFFER FROM THOSE
ADVERTISED IN THE TEXT OR ELSEWHERE.

THE PRICES SHOWN BELOW WERE CORRECT AT THE TIME OF GOING
TO PRESS (NOVEMBER '82)

☐	11993 8	**Up to Scratch**	*Diana Cooper* £1.50
☐	11364 6	**Animal Hotel**	*Diana Cooper* £1.50
☐	12014 6	**Any Fool Can Be a Dairy Farmer**	*James Robertson* £1.50
☐	10127 3	**One For Sorrow**	*Joyce Stranger* 85p
☐	11951 2	**Three's a Pack**	*Joyce Stranger* £1.50
☐	09893 0	**Breed of Giants**	*Joyce Stranger* 85p
☐	09462 5	**Lakeland Vet**	*Joyce Stranger* 70p
☐	11803 6	**How To Own a Sensible Dog**	*Joyce Stranger* £1.25
☐	12044 8	**The Monastery Cat and Other Animals**	*Joyce Stranger* £1.50
☐	10126 5	**Rusty**	*Joyce Stranger* £1.50
☐	10125 7	**Casey**	*Joyce Stranger* £1.50
☐	09892 2	**Zara**	*Joyce Stranger* £1.50
☐	10685 2	**Flash**	*Joyce Stranger* £1.50
☐	10695 X	**Kym**	*Joyce Stranger* £1.50

*All these books are available at your bookshop or newsagent, or can be ordered direct from the
publisher. Just tick the titles you want and fill in the form below.*

CORGI BOOKS, Cash Sales Department, P.O. Box 11, Falmouth, Cornwall.
Please send cheque or postal order, no currency.

Please allow cost of book(s) plus the following for postage and packing:

U.K. CUSTOMERS. 45p for the first book, 20p for the second book and 14p for each
additional book ordered, to a maximum charge of £1.63.

B.F.P.O. & EIRE. Please allow 45p for the first book, 20p for the second book plus 14p
per copy for the next three books, thereafter 8p per book.

OVERSEAS CUSTOMERS. Please allow 75p for the first book plus 21p per copy for
each additional book.

NAME (Block letters) ....

ADDRESS ....

....